An Unlikely Bride

Lelia M. Silver

Silver Summer Publishing

DEDICATION

To my nephew, Tristden, who has always been more of a little brother to me than a nephew. I hope you reach your dreams.

ACKNOWLEDGMENTS

This book would never have gotten this far without the support and encouragement of my husband and several dear friends and family members. My deepest thanks go to all of you. My thanks also go out to all those who have taken a chance and read my works. Your support and encouraging words are more appreciated than you can know. In addition, I must acknowledge the brilliance of Jane Austen. Her characters, plots, and settings are unparalleled. Anything that appears familiar within these pages can be attributed to her.

Lady Catherine was extremely indignant on the marriage of her nephew; and as she gave way to all the genuine frankness of her character, in her reply to the letter which announced its arrangement, she sent him language so very abusive, especially of Elizabeth, that for some time all intercourse was at an end. But at length, by Elizabeth's persuasion, he was prevailed on to overlook the offence, and seek a reconciliation;
– Pride and Prejudice

CHAPTER ONE

Colonel Richard Fitzwilliam crumpled the missive his butler had delivered only moments before and seriously considered the merits of tossing it in the fire burning in the hearth.

He was tired of being ordered about. It was one of the many reasons why he had sold his commission, retired, and now resided at his family's townhouse in London. He eyed the roaring fire. It would give him immense satisfaction to see the flames devour the rudely worded note. He had received many commands over his years in the military, but none of them had ever come close to the imperious tone of his Aunt Catherine's summons.

He sighed and rubbed his forehead. Unfortunately, he did not have the luxury of ignoring his aunt's missive. His family expected him to wait upon her, if for nothing else than to preserve the peace.

His cousin Darcy had married only a few months before, and his aunt had not made the adjustment well. She had always expected a match between Darcy and her own daughter, Anne. To have her daughter's position stolen by a young upstart like Elizabeth Bennet had been a serious blow for the older woman.

There had been rumors Lady Catherine had taken to her bed ill for three weeks. Fitzwilliam did not put much stock in those rumors. He could no more imagine his aunt taking to her bed than he could imagine Darcy married to the quiet, sensible Anne. He thought it far more likely she had flown into a rage that even her supercilious parson, Mr. Collins, would have been hard-pressed to bring her out of.

Of course, he had not been around Rosings at the time to know the truth. In all likelihood, the only person who knew the true nature of his aunt's reaction was his cousin Anne. Considering her poor health and retiring nature, he was unlikely to get more than a generic account of what had transpired from her. Anne had always been cowed by her more aggressive mother.

It was why he had always thought she and Darcy would be completely unsuitable for one another, not that anyone cared about his opinion on the matter. On the other hand, Elizabeth Darcy had all the fire and intelligence to match Darcy tit for tat. Fitzwilliam smiled to himself. Now that was the sort of match he would not mind for himself.

However, with Darcy out of the picture, thanks to his insistence that Aunt Catherine accept his new bride, which was something she had no intention of doing, Fitzwilliam was left on his own to see to the annual review of his aunt's estates. And if the tone of her letter was any indication, she expected Fitzwilliam to attend her post-haste.

Resigning himself to the idea, Fitzwilliam smoothed out the crumpled paper and ran his fingers over the ridges he had put in the crisp parchment as he read his aunt's directives one more time.

She expected him at Rosings in one week. It would be difficult to get his affairs arranged in time to make that deadline, but not impossible.

He stood to ring for the butler. There was no time like the present to get to work.

*****

One week later, Fitzwilliam turned his horse down the lane that led to Rosings. His mount slowed as they neared the parsonage, as if he, too, was reluctant to arrive at their destination.

Fitzwilliam reached out to pat the animal's neck with one gloved hand and chuckled. "It is only for a little while," he reassured the old chap. They had been through a lot together, he and Andronicus. This was just one more battle to be fought and won, one more field to conquer.

The horse snorted, as if he did not believe him.

Fitzwilliam shook his head. "Really. We shall be here a fortnight tops, less if Darcy left the books in good order. Last year we were done in record time." He smiled a little to himself. "Although we might have Elizabeth Bennet to thank for that."

Andronicus bobbed his head in agreement and then let out a welcoming whinny that made Fitzwilliam crane his head around to see what had caught the stallion's fancy. He grinned as he caught sight of his cousin, climbing into her pony cart in front of the parsonage. The parson's wife was expecting a child soon. No doubt Anne had been sent to help Mrs. Collins with preparations for the baby.

She had not yet noticed his arrival. He took a moment to survey her as she settled into the cart and picked up the reins. She looked well. Healthier than he had seen her in years. There was color in her cheeks and a luster to her hair that had been missing before. Why, she was almost beautiful in her own sort of way.

He would never have believed it possible. Surrounded by her overbearing mother and the dark furnishings of Rosings, Anne had always seemed a little drab and rundown. He had rarely seen her in the bright light of a sunny day and he was amazed by the transformation in her.

As he watched, she lifted her face to the sun and smiled, the simple gesture transforming her features. He did not think he had ever seen someone so content and at peace as she was. At that moment, she was not just almost beautiful. She was downright breathtaking. No other woman of his acquaintance could compare to her.

Shocked, he did not even realize he had reined his mount to a standstill. Why had he never noticed this side of his cousin? Had he really been so oblivious to her? To his chagrin, he realized he had never really given her a second thought, much less a second glance.

His last visit to Rosings had been eclipsed by the obvious chemistry between Darcy and Elizabeth. Prior to that, he had always been so busy avoiding Lady Catherine and riding the estate with Darcy that he had only ever spent a few hours over dinner with his cousin.

He just might have to change that.

She lifted her hands to shake the reins over her pony's back, reminding him he was still standing in the middle of the lane, gawking at her. He closed his mouth and goaded Andronicus into motion, calling out with a cheerful grin, "Hello, Cousin!"

She turned at the sound of his voice to spy him coming up the lane toward her and rewarded him for the greeting with a heartfelt smile. "Cousin Richard! What a pleasant surprise! Mother and I were not expecting you to arrive until this evening."

He reined in his mount beside her cart. "I managed to make good time on the roads, thanks to my faithful steed here."

Andronicus shook his head prettily, making his mane fly, and preened.

Anne laughed, a lovely sound Richard could not remember ever hearing before. Then again, who could laugh in Aunt Catherine's company? She would surely reprimand them for the unseemly display. He grinned, enjoying the slightly rebellious act even more so because it was Anne that had done it.

His lovely cousin was not at all what he had expected.

Anne reached out to pet Andronicus' nose, her calm touch stilling the restless animal. "He is a fine gentleman, much like his owner."

Richard tried not to let his own chest puff up at her praise. "Thank you, Cousin. I am not sure your mother would agree with you, but the sentiment is appreciated- by both Andronicus and me."

Anne picked up the lines again. "Speaking of my mother, she has enlisted Cook's help to make all your favorite dishes tonight. I think she is determined to win you over to her side since Darcy went against her wishes." Her mouth twitched, but it was her eyes that gave away her humor with the situation.

He grimaced. "Spare me, please. I am only here to do my duty."

The smile dancing in her eyes disappeared and her spine straightened, making him instantly regret his hastily spoken words. "Of course. I would not expect otherwise. You have always been most responsible when it comes to your familial duties. Mother and I appreciate your diligence, especially since the entirety of the work will fall to you this year." She glanced at Rosings, just visible through the trees.

"Mother will be expecting me. I must be going." Her gaze was disappointed as she slapped the reins over the pony's back, as if she thought she had gained an ally and then had him stolen away from her.

He sighed and watched her pull away. "Not much of a gentleman now, am I, Andronicus?"

The horse snorted his agreement, crooking Richard's mouth into a half smile. "Well, you need not have been so vehement."

The horse bobbed his head, as if to say it had been absolutely necessary. Richard had to admit, the horse was probably right.

"Do not worry, old chap. I am man enough to know when I should apologize." He kicked the horse into a trot, catching up to Anne's cart quickly.

She glanced at him from the corner of her eye but otherwise did not acknowledge him. He resisted the urge to sigh. She was not going to make this easy for him.

He did not wait for her to make eye contact. "Anne, I do apologize. I spoke without thinking and I do not wish for you to misconstrue my statement. I simply meant that I have no wish to be courted or manipulated by your mother. My feelings toward her are no reflection of my feelings toward you. Indeed, I find I barely know you, Cousin. Tell me, what news is there at Rosings?"

For an instant, he thought she was going to refuse to be reconciled, but then she relented, throwing him a small smile. Her shoulders relaxed. "There is not much news to tell. The winter was difficult, but now that spring is upon us I find myself looking forward to the change in weather and circumstances. Mrs. Collins has been a great companion to me these many months since Mrs. Jenkins left me. I think you will find her presence in the dining room to be very refreshing."

It was perhaps the longest speech Richard had ever heard his cousin utter, and he was not entirely sure how to respond. He did not wish to risk offending her again by stating his true opinion, yet he could not quite keep the skepticism out of his voice. "I have no doubt."

To his surprise, she chuckled. "You may keep your doubts, Cousin, but I take whatever small favors are granted me. Mrs. Collins is a welcome voice of reason around the table, although too often her words are discarded by the other guests. My mother is not the only one who likes to hear herself speak."

Flabbergasted by her forthright speech, Richard could not find a response. It was all he could do to close his gaping mouth.

She sent him a smile that dimpled her cheek becomingly. "You are shocked I see. It is not easy to have our closely held expectations challenged. It was Mrs. Darcy's greatest fault. She was forever challenging Mother. Yet, I cannot fault her when I have longed to do the same myself. I simply accept that should I wish to enjoy a peaceful existence in the same house as my mother, I must choose when to hold my tongue and when to let it loose. My mother is not all bad, Richard, despite what you have experienced." It was the first time she had called him simply by his given name.

Richard was silent for a moment before turning a contemplative gaze on her. "It seems nothing is as I expected it to be, Anne, least of all you. I shall look forward to having any further expectations challenged."

He tipped his hat to her and took the fork in the road that led to the front door, where he would be expected to present himself.

She steered her pony and cart around the back of the house to the stables, smiling a little to herself. Fitzwilliam was not the only one who had discovered his expectations were quite mistaken. She found herself just as eager as he was to see what other wrong assumptions she had made about her cousin.

*****

Anne entered the house through the back door. Her mother would have been appalled to find her using the servants' entrance, but Anne rather enjoyed entering through the warm kitchen, bustling with activity. It reminded her that not all at Rosings was as it appeared on the surface.

The servants had looked at her askance the first few times she had dared to do it, but now they were as accustomed to her presence as they were to the long worktable that ran the length of the room. It helped that Anne had long ago perfected the art of fading into the background.

Today, the downstairs was even more abuzz with activity than usual, thanks to the arrival of their guest. Cook and her assistants were busy preparing all of Richard's favorite foods, thanks to the cook at his parent's townhouse, who had been convinced to send round his recipes. Anne was not sure what her mother had written in her note to convince the man, but she knew her mother well enough to send a note of her own with her profuse thanks and some monetary compensation for the man's help.

She had personally overseen the preparations to Richard's room. The chamber she had chosen for his stay was different than the one he had previously used, and she hoped he would not question the change. She had moved him to one of Rosings' finest apartments, where the draft did not reach and the morning light warmed the rather sterile space. It was the perfect space to work in, and if she was honest with herself, she rather coveted that apartment.

Her own rooms, while warm, thanks to her mother's insistence on her care for her health, were closed off and closeted away so the noise of the household would not disturb her rest. In addition, they were entirely too close to her mother's rooms for her comfort.

Change was a difficult prospect for her mother, so Anne had yet to broach the topic of changing rooms. In time, perhaps, she might be able to make the move. In the meantime, she was content to bide her time until her mother was ready to hear about it.

Still, she hoped Richard would enjoy the space. It was a shame to have it sit empty all the time when it could be in use. Anne liked to imagine Rosings the way she thought her ancestors had meant for it to be when they built it, full of light and laughter, with the sound of children's feet running through the halls.

Anne had never run in the halls. She would never have dared to risk her mother's sharp tongue. But she rather thought her father had in his childhood. Or if not him, then surely this house had once been filled with a happy family.

Sometimes she would walk the gallery in the back hall of the house and wonder about the people in the portraits that lined the walls. Would she have liked them? Would they have smiled at her as a child and applauded her efforts on the pianoforte? Would they have enthused over how beautiful she was as she made her debut in London?

Those were all experiences she would never have. Her mother liked to say she would have been proficient on the pianoforte if she had ever learned, but her mother's concern about her health had kept her from the instrument. Sitting at the pianoforte for hours of practice would have been too taxing. Her nerves could not have handled the mistakes. Excuses abounded.

By the time Anne reached the age when she might have entered society, Lady Catherine had discovered that her importance in Kent far out shadowed any influence she might have in Town. She never even mentioned a possibility of Anne going to London for her debut. Anne secretly thought her mother had realized taking her to London would have meant relinquishing her hold on her. So Anne had resigned herself to Rosings and the life she had there. In time, instead of resenting her entrapment, she had begun to enjoy it and to look for ways to enliven her dreary existence.

She had succeeded. Her contentment here was complete. Still, she had always looked forward to the visit of her cousins and the news they brought of the outside world. Last year had been the most exciting of all, with the arrival of Mrs. Collins, and subsequently Elizabeth Bennet, now Darcy.

Anne had always known she was never bound to become the future Mrs. Darcy, despite what her mother might assert. As soon as she had met Elizabeth Bennet, and saw how her cousin mooned over her, she had known Darcy had found his match. It had just taken her cousin a little longer to come around to the idea.

This year, there was a different sort of excitement at Rosings. Mrs. Collins was expecting a baby, and while that did mean Anne was often deprived of her company around the dinner table, it gave her a wonderful excuse to get out of the house and visit Mrs. Collins at the parsonage, as she had been doing earlier when Richard had come upon her.

Of course, that also meant her mother was taking a keen interest in all the happenings at the parsonage, and she would expect a full report now that Anne had returned.

Anne skirted the main rooms of the house, her mother's strident voice reaching her as she walked the back hallways to her room. She shook her head, a small smile on her face as she imagined Fitzwilliam in the drawing room with her mother, patiently listening as she expounded on one topic or another. The poor, long-suffering man. He really was too good to them. Once inside her chambers, her maid helped her out of her driving clothes and into something her mother would find more suitable for entertaining guests.

Then she was back in the hallways again, heading to the drawing room and her mother. And Richard Fitzwilliam. She must not forget the welcome light he was in the household. That thought had her entering the drawing room with a smile.

Her mother perked up at the sight of her, interrupting her own monologue to say, "Ah! Anne! There you are! Richard told me he ran into you outside the parsonage. How is the dear Mrs. Collins today?"

Anne took her seat on the settee and spared her cousin a glance. "She is as well as can be expected, I suppose. She is rather uncomfortable, but looking forward to the blessed event, which is drawing ever nearer. She will make a fine mother, I am sure."

Lady Catherine harrumphed. "She would be a sight more comfortable if she took to her bed as I advised."

Anne responded, "Mrs. Collins prefers to be active in serving her husband's parishioners, which I applaud. You must admit, Mother, that her presence in the parish would be sorely missed if she were to take to her bed as you suggested."

Her mother waved away her response. "Yes, yes. She is a hard worker, I will grant you that much. It was very well done of Mr. Collins to be so exact in following my instructions when he picked out his wife. He could hardly have found someone else so well suited for the job. I for one quite congratulate myself on a job well done."

Anne resisted the urge to roll her eyes but noticed that Fitzwilliam was not quite as successful. He hid his snort of laughter behind his hand.

Lady Catherine immediately honed in on the sound. "Was that a cough, young man? Are you ill?" She frowned at him. "You know we cannot have any illness in this household. Anne's health is too precarious."

This time, she could not prevent the eye roll. Thankfully, her mother's full attention was focused on Richard so she did notice. Richard, however, did. His mouth twitched. "I assure you, I am not ill, Aunt Catherine. I simply had something stuck in my throat. I would never jeopardize Anne's health; although I must say that she is looking remarkably well. I would not guess that her health has been a struggle recently."

Anne gave him a smile for his support and the sweet compliment. No one had ever told her she looked remarkably well. No one had ever actually given her a compliment, period. She found it felt nice. Really nice, actually.

Lady Catherine sniffed. "Not recently, per say, but you know she has always had a weak constitution. I do not want her to suffer a relapse when she is finally feeling somewhat well."

Her mother's insistence on her ill health was annoying, especially when she had not been sick in ages, but Anne tried to concentrate on the well-meaning behind her overprotectiveness. She smiled at the room in general. "The sunshine has done wonders for my constitution. I have been greatly enjoying my visits to Mrs. Collins." And with that, the conversation was brought neatly back around to Mrs. Collins.

"I am quite convinced they shall have a son," Lady Catherine said, quickly diving back into one of her favorite topics. "I told Mr. Collins so just the other day. He must have a son. Then I shall be assured that Kent will be left in good hands when he is ready to retire from his post. I told him he must make his sermon this Sunday on the blessings of children and sons in particular. I myself was never granted the gift of a son, but I am quite grateful that I shall have Anne to look after me in my old age. You will never leave me, will you, Anne? It would quite break my heart to have her situated far away from me."

Anne kept her gaze trained on her folded hands and tried not to fidget in her seat. Her mother could spot dissension from a mile away. "You need not worry about that, Mother. I have no plans to marry and move away at the present time." Indeed, she had no such prospects. Her mother had scared away any young man that might have attempted to come calling years ago. Anne was inclined to believe she had done so purposefully, either in a bid to keep her daughter near or to keep the way clear for Darcy.

Lady Catherine nodded. "It is too bad, really. I would so like grandchildren to spoil. Just the idea of having the Collins' little boy running around has made me long for a little one in this house."

Anne and Richard shared an uncomfortable glance. A wistful Lady Catherine was an enigma. Neither he nor she knew quite how to respond.

Then the wistful look on her face twisted into anger. "It is too bad that hussy Elizabeth Bennet stole Darcy away from you. If you had married him and united our two estates, I might have had a grandchild on the way by now. Instead, that silly Mrs. Bennet shall have that honor!"

Anne was rendered speechless by her outburst, but Fitzwilliam was not. He coughed discreetly into his hand. "I believe Mrs. Bennet will have some time to wait for that honor. Regardless, I am sure you would not wish your nephew ill, Aunt Catherine." He smiled his most charming smile, the one that had won him more than one argument in the battlefield of London Society. "I should hate to lose your favor if I should ever marry. You are my favorite aunt after all."

Lady Catherine sniffed. "I am your only living aunt, Richard. Do not try to placate me with clever sayings. It shall not work." Still, she softened. "I am sure that when you do marry you shall make some woman a fine husband. You have never shirked your responsibility to me. Unlike some people we shall not name."

They did not need to be named. Everyone in the room knew who she was talking about. Anne sighed and tried to redirect the conversation to a more productive topic. "Mrs. Collins mentioned that one of the families in the village has been experiencing a leaky roof. I thought it might be wise to have one of the servants go down and see about repairing it. What do you think, Mother?"

Lady Catherine, as always, was eager to share her opinion, and waxed so poetic on the subject that she had still not exhausted the topic by the time they went in to dine.

In fact, she waxed so long and heartily on the subject that she had quite exhausted herself by the time dinner was finished. Anne, sensing Lady Catherine's flagging energy with wisdom born from experience, suggested her mother take herself to bed so that she might be at her best in the morning, when she was to receive Mr. Collins.

Her mother took her advice, leaving Anne and Fitzwilliam to entertain each other in the drawing room. As this was much preferable to allowing Lady Catherine to entertain them, Fitzwilliam did not complain. In fact, he was rather eager to have some time alone with his cousin. She had already surprised him with her beauty, humor, and deft handling of Lady Catherine; he wondered now what other surprises she held in store.

She did not disappoint. As Richard settled into one arm chair, she went to a small desk in the corner of the room and riffled through the contents before pulling out a single sheet of paper.

Paper in hand, she took a seat in the armchair across from his. He watched her curiously, expecting her to share the contents of that note, but instead she simply folded the paper into quarters and laid it on her lap, seemingly content to make him wait.

The inefficiencies of the military should have taught Fitzwilliam patience, but he found that virtue deserting him at the moment. He gestured to the paper she held. "What is that?"

"A list," she answered calmly.

"A list?" he asked.

She nodded.

"Is it for me?"

"I suppose so," she told him.

"What does that mean?" he asked.

She shrugged. "Mother insisted I draw up an accounting of all you and Darcy usually see to while you are here to review the estate. She thought it might be useful to have since this time you shall have to carry Darcy's portion of the work in addition to your own. She did not wish you to forget anything." She glanced at the paper in her hand and added, "I rather thought you also might not wish to forget anything and risk having to return later when my mother discovers it."

Richard could not help chuckling. "You are a wise woman, Anne de Bourgh."

She smiled. "Not wise. Just prepared."

He shook his head. "A rose by any other name…" He held out his hand for the list. "May I see that?"

With a reluctance that confused him, she handed it over. Richard unfolded the sheet, smoothing out the ridges she had created when she folded it, and held it up to the lamp so he could read the writing. It was long and thorough, and Richard was confident that there were items on the list neither he nor Darcy had ever done. Still, he could see the need for every item listed, and found himself determined to see it through to completion. Satisfied, he folded the note back up and slipped it into his pocket for safekeeping.

Anne was eyeing him warily. "So, what do you think, Cousin?"

He smiled at her. "I think it is ambitious, but practical. There is nothing on this list that cannot be done, and nothing that should not be done. It is well-thought out. I shall begin tomorrow morning by going over the books with your steward. That will give me a more complete picture with which to assess the status of the estate."

To his surprise and consternation, she relaxed into her chair, relief passing over her features. He thought the expression a rather strange overreaction to his statement. It was odd that she would have such a strong emotional attachment to that list. How would she have reacted if he had been derogatory?

She did not give him time to dwell on the subject. "Our steward will be happy to have you on hand. He has been singing your praises for weeks. I think it is one of the many factors that motivated my mother to write to you."

Considering that Richard had only had limited interaction with the steward in the past, since that duty mostly fell to Darcy, he found that statement surprising. Richard was an outdoors man, given more to roaming the countryside than going over numbers while he was in Kent.

Then again, if the man had been forced to deal with Lady Catherine in the months since he and Darcy had been in Kent, he could well understand the man's anticipation of their return.

Unfortunately, now all of the duties, even the ones he found most onerous, fell on his shoulders since Darcy was no longer welcome at Rosings. He tapped his fingers against his leg in a rapid staccato. "I sincerely doubt he has need of my services. These last few years, the estate has been running in superb condition. It has quite improved."

"I am very pleased to hear you say that." Anne beamed at him, her smile far outweighing the compliment. One might have thought he was complimenting her, not her mother and steward.

His consternation must have shown, for she quickly schooled her features into a more subdued expression. She cleared her throat. "It is always good to know that the estate will go on caring for our needs, especially as Mother has grown older and requires more assistance."

Richard smiled and shook his head. "As long as Mr. Collins is around, I think your mother will be quite content."

Anne laughed, a delightful sound that filled his heart with warmth. How had he lived this long and not known that joy? Laughter was such a precious commodity in this house. He was glad he could be the one to bring out that joy in her.

She rested her head in one palm, turning her warm gaze on him as the firelight flickered over her face, alternately hiding and highlighting her features. "Without Mr. Collins there would be no Mrs. Collins or baby Collins, and so I cannot complain. There has been more life at Rosings since they came than there has been for years."

Her voice turned wistful. "Your visits have always been the only other bright spots." Then she seemed to shake herself out of her melancholy with a wide grin. "We shall see if you can live up to the hype this year without your accomplice. I daresay it will not be as exciting as last year. Tell me, how are Mr. and Mrs. Darcy? Surely, you have heard from them?"

The light in Anne's eyes told him she did not harbor any ill will toward their cousin and his new wife, unlike her mother. She was watching him expectantly, hoping for news. He could not bear to disappoint her. "They are doing well. Mrs. Darcy is settling in wonderfully at Pemberley. Darcy adores her, Georgiana is emboldened by her, and the staff is captivated. She is a fine mistress. Georgiana will learn much from her."

She smiled broadly. "I am pleased to hear that. I knew she and Darcy were well-matched. It was only a matter of time before they realized it for themselves. He is so very different when he is comfortable among family."

Richard nodded. "The effect is only enhanced now that he is married. He is fortunate she learned his true personality before he scared her off forever. He had not endeared himself to her when they were here last."

"No, but it was the beginning of a turning point. They needed only time and opportunity for their love to grow." That assessing gaze, which had so easily seen past Darcy's foibles, turned on him. "And how about you, Richard? What news do you have?"

He was not as comfortable now that her focus was on him. "I have sold my commission, as you may be aware."

She nodded. "Yes. Your mother wrote mine when word of that reached her. She was very surprised."

He sighed. "She very well may have been. I was surprised."

That statement prompted her to cock her head and look at him questioningly. "What brought about the change?"

He shrugged. "It was not a life I wanted anymore. There was too much worry and responsibility. I could not bear the thought of going to war again. After a while, I found taking orders to be burdensome and I no longer needed the prominence to feel secure in my position. It was time to let it go and seek other avenues. I do not have the wealth Darcy does, nor will I ever, but my future is secure between my family's holdings and my own."

She nodded, commenting sagely, "Contentment is a fine quality, Richard, and one I have found most helpful. Wealth does not equate happiness, as we both well know."

He could only agree with her. "It is the truth."

She shifted in her seat. "How did your parents handle the news?"

A corner of his mouth turned up. "My mother found it necessary to write to her sister, did she not? I think they were shocked, but have been supportive for the most part. I think Mother is relieved to no longer be constantly worried about my safety."

"I think that was a relief for the entire family," Anne admitted. "I know I rejoiced when I heard the news." A smile spread across her face. "I was also very pleased to know I would not have to be the one to audit the books this year."

Richard chuckled. "I very much doubt your mother would ever ask you to do that."

She snorted, in a very unladylike fashion that Richard found surprisingly delightful. "Ask? No. Demand? Perhaps."

The clock in the hall struck the hour and they both started in surprise at the time. Anne rose in a swirl of skirts. "Forgive me, Cousin. I had no idea how late it had grown.

You have traveled a long way today. I must not keep you from your rest."

Richard stood, strangely loath to leave, even though his body had begun to protest the lateness of the hour some time ago. "Do not blame yourself, Anne. I have had a wonderful time catching up with you. I only regret that your steward will keep me very busy in the days to come. We shall have very little time to spend together."

A corner of her mouth turned up. "Not too busy for a little light-hearted entertainment, I hope. Mother has requested that you join us for a dinner party she is hosting later in the week."

"I shall look forward to it." He bowed over her hand. "Mayhap the books will be in good order and I shall see more of you than I expect."

She smiled genially. "One can hope." She curtseyed and turned to go up to her room. "Good night, Cousin."

Richard watched her go, although he was the one who should have claimed fatigue long ago and retired. His valet was surely waiting up for him. Yet, he could not bring himself to abandon the room where Anne had come to life.

Rosings was not precisely the hostile environment he had always thought it to be. Even his rooms this time around were warm and inviting, and he could not help but wonder if his cousin had been the source of that welcome surprise as well.

From everything he was learning about her, it seemed to fit. Certainly, he had never felt so at home within the walls of Rosings; no, nor in the whole of Kent. His ready good nature usually stood him in good stead here, along with a healthy dose of the outdoors, but he wondered if another tactic might not be even more useful for his sanity. Or rather, another person.

He had told Anne he was unlikely to see much of her while he was here, but he heartily hoped that it did not turn out to be the case. If he had anything to do with it, it would not. While he normally dreaded Aunt Catherine's dinner parties, he found himself looking forward to the opportunity to be with Anne again.

Sometimes, change was good.

The prospect alive in his mind, he went upstairs to find his bed, whistling jauntily.

CHAPTER TWO

It seemed Anne had been keeping another secret from him.

Richard stared at the steward sitting across from him, dumbfounded. He closed his gaping mouth with a snap. "Excuse me. I do not believe I heard you correctly. Could you please repeat yourself?"

The steward frowned at him, but obliged. "Miss de Bourgh has been handling all the finances and bookkeeping. She has almost singled-handedly been running Rosings these past two years. With help from me, of course."

Richard slumped into his seat, suddenly overcome. His explanation certainly explained a lot about his interaction the night before with Anne. Now he understood why she had taken his reaction to the list and records so personally.

He ran a hand over his face, rubbing the grit out of his eyes from staring at line after line of figures for hours on end. He tore his hand away suddenly as it occurred to him that Anne had likely done the same thing many times. "That was not what I expected to hear."

The steward regarded him warily. "She has been doing a fine job of it. Surely, you can see that for yourself. The numbers prove it."

Richard knew he was making the man defensive, which would not help the situation. He hastened to reassure him, "I do see that. The estate has not been this profitable in years. I am simply surprised. I had no inclination that Miss de Bourgh had a hand in running the estate. My cousin, Mr. Darcy, gave me no clue this situation might exist."

It was not like Darcy to keep him out of the loop. Still, even though Darcy was younger than him, his cousin had been managing his estate, Pemberley, for years. Richard, being the younger son, had never been trained for the task. He could understand why Darcy would have made such a decision without consulting him. It was simply irksome now that Darcy was not around to have such things sprung upon him.

"It was to be on a trial basis only," the steward explained. "However, at the conclusion of his visit last year, Mr. Darcy gave his approval for the arrangement to continue. He seemed to think it was in the best interests of all involved. I was led to believe that you, too, had been consulted in his decision."

"I am not contending that it was not the right decision to make. Indeed, it seems to be working out rather well. I simply wish I had been informed as you supposed I had been." He rubbed at his eyes again. "I think it is time for a break from the ledgers. If you will excuse, I am going to take a ride."

He pushed back his seat and rose without waiting for the steward to nod his approval. Richard needed some time and space to process this information before he could proceed any farther. On Andronicus' back he would find it. He always seemed to do his best thinking on horseback.

In short order, he had changed into his riding clothes and had Andronicus brought around. The horse greeted him with a warm whicker, nipping at the hat on his head. Richard deftly moved out of reach, swinging himself into the saddle. "Not right now, old boy. I am not in the mood for games."

The horse shook his head and snorted.

Richard chuckled. "I know. You do not care. Well, come on then. Let us get a move on and see if we can run off some of your energy." He turned the horse down one of the many paths crisscrossing the estate. At one time or another, he had traversed most of them, and he happened to know that this particular one would take him up by the old greenhouse and gardener's cottage to a nice level field where he could push Andronicus to a gallop and let off some steam.

As Rosings disappeared behind them, Richard urged Andronicus to a fast trot. He was not sure why the prospect of Anne running the estate bothered him. He was not even sure what he might do about it. It was true she had been doing a good job running it; he was not certain he would have done so well in her place. Still, handling all the estate business was a large job for any one person, much less a young woman with uncertain health.

Although, he reminded himself, Anne did not seem to be in as bad of health as her mother made her out to be. By her own account, she was feeling quite well. If the work she had done on the estate was any indication, she was telling the truth. Could he really take all of that away from her simply because of society's expectations? Was he the sort of man that refused to give a woman the chance to do a job just because it was usually relegated to a man?

The prospect that he might bothered him more than it would have most men.

Darcy had not been that way, obviously, and Richard found he could neither take that privilege away from Anne, nor could he not let the omission pass without some comment. She needed to know that he knew. She also deserved to know that she was doing a good job.

Richard had almost made up his mind to turn his mount around and do just that when a brush of black against the side of the old greenhouse caught his eye. He turned his head to give it his full attention, hauling in Andronicus unceremoniously as he realized it was Anne's cart and pony.

The pony was unharnessed, grazing in a patch of grass at the side of the building. It was the cart that had caught his eye, resting against the greenhouse. If her cart and pony were here, where was Anne?

The last time he had been out this way, which admittedly was several years ago, the greenhouse had been overgrown and abandoned. Now, the area had been cleaned up and repairs made. He wondered if it had been put back into use by the gardener. Even if that was so, what was Anne doing there?

He would have to investigate. Andronicus perked up at the sight of the other animal, sounding a welcome that brought the other horse's head up. Richard shook his head and nudged his mount toward the greenhouse. If all the noise did not give away their presence, he did not know what would.

Sure enough, Anne appeared in the doorway, raising a hand over her eyes to see him in the bright sunlight. Her smile disappeared quickly as she got a good look at his serious visage.

She came to hold Andronicus' bridle, words spilling from her mouth. "What is the matter? Is something wrong? What has happened? Is it Mother?"

Her worry made him smile, although he could not have said why. Perhaps it was the knowledge that she would have been asking those same questions about him if it had been another person on Andronicus.

His smile confused her. He could tell by the way she furrowed her brow and bit back anything else she might have said. He slid from his mount, coming around to Andronicus' head to take his bridle from her. "I did not expect to find you out here. Is there a Mrs. Collins near the gardener you plan to visit?"

His quiet teasing was at odds with his serious gaze. Anne pondered him thoughtfully before answering. "No. There is no Mrs. Collins. The greenhouse is my own private refuge. I had it fixed up a few years ago, when I started feeling better, and it has done much for my well-being."

Her statement piqued his curiosity. "What do you do out here?"

She smiled, contentment and joy stealing over her features. "Why do you not come inside and see?"

Intrigued, Richard accepted the invitation. "It would be my pleasure." He looped Andronicus' reins around the hitching post by the door and followed her inside the glass building.

The humidity inside the building had obscured his view of the contents from the outside, but the transformation from its deteriorated state only a few years ago was staggering. The space was filled with rows upon rows of rose bushes. Every variety he could name and many he could not blossomed around him, showering the space with beauty and fragrance.

He paused to take it all in, inhaling the sweet aroma. When he looked down at Anne again, she was grinning up at him. He smiled back at her and said, "I can see why you claim this as your refuge. I do not think there is a rival in all of Kent. Your gardener is excellent."

Her brow puckered. "This is not the work of our gardener, although you are correct. He is excellent. This space is reserved for me. These roses are mine."

He looked around him again, this time really taking in all the work she had done. "This is all your handiwork? My compliments, milady. You have worked marvels. I would never have guessed such a petite and unlikely source of such beauty, but I suppose I should have known. Beauty begets beauty."

His compliment eased her frown. "It was a logical conclusion, I suppose. Come, let me show you of what I am particularly proud."

He followed her down the rows to a corner that had obviously been set aside for a specific use. The rose bushes there were newer, younger, but his uneducated eye could discern no noticeable difference from the other plants, although her pride in them was evident.

She stood for a moment, waiting for him to comment, but he just cocked his head and looked at her. She smiled and shook her head, discerning his confusion. "These are my own unique variety. I crossbred two species to get this particular shade of coral. I hope to have it verified and recorded someday, once I have made sure of its hardiness."

Richard looked at her and then looked at the plants, and then back at her. "You bred these?"

She lifted her chin and straightened her spine as though preparing to take offense. "I did. Are they not beautiful?"

"They are," he acknowledged. "I had no idea you possessed such a talent in addition to your many others."

His statement caught her attention. She drew her brows together in confusion. "Of what other talents do you speak?"

Rocking back on his heels, he tucked his hands in his pockets and watched her face closely. "Why, your talent for handling an estate. Your steward this morning was very informative. I had no idea you had taken over managing the property."

Guilt crossed her face, confirming what he already knew. He spoke before she could. "You should have told me last night. You had the opportunity."

"I should have," she acknowledged. "Yet, you did not know. How was I to know Darcy had not told you? And then, if he had not told you, who was I to say you should be told? To be honest, I quite expected you to ride in, take everything off my hands, and forbid me from having any authority any longer."

"I could do that," he said. "One word to your mother would suffice." He waited for her response, wondering how she would react to the perceived threat and hating that she might think him such a man.

She bit her lip and looked away and Richard could not bear to let her think he might do that any longer.

He added, "However, I cannot in good conscience remove you from a position you are obviously quite adept at filling. Rosings has not seen such good management in decades. Your steward is impressed and I am, too. You, Cousin, have quite the head for business. My brother would be jealous of your prowess, for he does not have near the head for figures you do."

The shock spreading across her face was priceless to see and more than made up for her bad opinion of him. She stuttered, "You…you mean you do not mind? Truly?"

He smiled down on her, feeling benevolent. "Truly. You are doing a good job. I see no reason to put someone else in charge. Your steward also mentioned that he appreciated your influence in keeping Lady Catherine involved in the community and shall we say, distracted, in the household. It has made his job quite a bit easier since you have taken over. I do not think he would consider giving up his post now."

"That is a relief," she told him. "I do not know how we would manage without him. He was very helpful in showing me how things were supposed to be run, and not at all condescending."

"Yes. He is a good man," Richard agreed. "And you run a tight ship. All of the servants are very efficient at their duties. What intrigues me the most is how you managed to keep all this from your mother. Did you not worry that she would find out and be angry about your deception?"

Anne shrugged and gave him a small smile. "I have found that sometimes it is easier to ask for forgiveness than permission, Richard, especially when it comes to my mother. What she does not know will not hurt her. In all honesty, it will probably only help her."

Richard nodded his agreement with her supposition. Her mother had certainly not been harmed by being kept out of the loop in this instance. Yet, he pondered her first statement. "Is there anything else you need to ask forgiveness for before I delve any deeper into my investigation?"

He thought she might pause and think over her response, but she simply smiled and said, "Nothing of which I am aware. I will inform you if I think of something."

He narrowed his eyes at her, wondering. "Just so you know, I prefer to have my information up front. You do not have to ask for my permission to take care of what belongs to you, but I would appreciate being kept informed. If you do so, you shall have no need to ask for forgiveness from me in the future." He paused. "I do notice you have not apologized for keeping information from me in the past."

She grinned. "I do not think it wise to apologize for something I am not sorry I did. It would be hypocritical of me, which is a quality I think you would hardly find endearing."

He could not help but laugh at her statement. "You are correct. Hypocrisy would not endear you to me. I have seen enough of that in my lifetime to last an eternity. I prefer your honesty."

"Then we shall get along splendidly," she told him. "For I have always wished I could be completely truthful and open with someone, and until now, I have not found anyone to whom I could trust that honor."

He was taken aback by her candor. She spoke of having no one with whom to be completely honest, yet she told him her thoughts so easily. What did that tell him about her? More importantly, what did that say about her feelings for him? Was her easy manner and honesty a front to put him at ease so *he* would speak more freely? Or did it spring from a realization that he was someone she could trust?

He did not dare to ask her outright. Not yet. He was not quite ready to match her candor. Her trust issues did not hold a candle to his. Especially since he had already discovered she had been withholding the truth from him. Still, he could not deny she had done so in good conscience. And she had been honest with him about her failure to apologize. He had to give her credit for that.

He told her casually, "You have the advantage over me. In the military the force with the higher ground often has the advantage. You have had the luxury of gaining the higher ground with your prior knowledge of the situation here. I am having to scramble to catch up."

She cocked her head at him. "Your illustration is faulty. We are not dueling armies at odds over a military campaign. We are on the same side, are we not?"

He smiled at her logic. "Perhaps. If we are to apply that logic, I would be a lowly foot soldier, waiting for information to be passed down from a superior. I am not sure I like that metaphor."

She grinned. "I see it bothers your male sensibilities."

He chuckled. "It does at that. Still, your illustration is more accurate than mine. I will not deny it. Despite evidence to the contrary, my male sensibilities do not keep me from admitting when I am wrong."

She grinned cheekily. "I am pleased to hear you say that. I am not sure our cousin, Mr. Darcy, would have been so quick to admit his faults. Indeed, if he had been, his romance with Elizabeth might have been far different and quite a bit simpler."

"Yes, but far less entertaining."

"It would be at that." She chuckled and moved away from her treasured plants, reaching for a watering can on a bench. "What plans do you have for the afternoon? Have you finished going over the ledgers?"

He shook his head and trailed her as she began painstakingly watering her roses one by one. "It will take more than one day to complete that task, and I am sorry to say that numbers do not come as easily to me as they do to you. I find it is best for all involved if I intersperse the time I spend with the books with more outdoor activities."

She nodded sympathetically. "I understand. I too find it difficult to be cooped up inside, especially when the weather is as fine as today."

"It is a fine day," he agreed. "I always find that a ride on Andronicus helps me to clear my mind. I was out doing that when I caught sight of your cart and pony. Do you come out here often?"

She nodded, set down the watering can, and picked up a pair of pruning shears. "Every day that the weather and my health allows. It is rare that estate business keeps me from the greenhouse. The steward knows he can find me here if he needs me."

"It is certainly a pleasant spot. I am happy I happened upon it, or I might never have learned of its existence."

Anne smiled to herself. "No. You would have found out sooner or later, if not from the steward, then from me."

He wondered at that, but did not comment.

Sensing his questions, she glanced at him. "My roses are very close to my heart. I doubt I would have been able to keep silent about them for long. They are my passion. Much as riding clears your mind, I find caring for my roses helps me when I am facing a difficult decision or simply need an excuse to be out of the house."

He nodded, suddenly understanding. "I see. I am glad you have such a release. I think everyone needs something that can do that for them. I know I find it an invaluable aid."

She nodded and hummed her agreement as she set to work pruning her roses. He watched her for a few moments longer, then picked up another pair of shears and hefted them up to her line of sight. "Would you like some help?"

She eyed him warily, apparently unsure if she should risk enlisting him. "I do not think that would be wise." She reached for the pruning shears. "It might be dangerous to our health. You should never point those towards anyone's eyes, including your own. They are very sharp."

Reluctantly, he let her tug them from his fingers. He shoved his hands back in his pockets. "You know I have handled more dangerous equipment than a pair of shears."

She barely spared him a glance, moving as she was between her plants. "Yes. However, you were properly trained on how to use those instruments before you were allowed to run rampant with them. Apparently, your training with gardening shears has been lacking."

He grinned slowly. "Yet, how can I be expected to use them properly without someone to teach me?"

She raised her eyes to look at him, startled. "What are you suggesting, Cousin?"

"I am simply suggesting that you might teach me what I need to know. It is apparent to me that you are as adept with your pruning shears as any soldier is with his musket."

She grimaced at his simile. "I am not sure I appreciate that comparison. I am no soldier."

"You used the illustration yourself only a few minutes ago. Are your delicate female sensibilities now enflamed?"

She laughed at his teasing. "No, my female sensibilities are hardier than your male ones. Come along then. If you insist on learning, you must be taught correctly."

She handed him the shears, this time showing him how to hold them correctly, and then led him through the aisles, explaining and teaching as she went. He knew there was more to caring for her roses than what she showed him; he had, after all, shown up after she had been there for a while. Still, she was patient and kind and dignified him with her responses to his questions. She was ever the lady. Yet, she smiled and teased and did not hesitate to speak her mind, especially when she knew more about the topic than he did.

Richard was content to be with her, to listen and learn and to get to know this woman a little better. There was still so much about her he did not know and he could not expect to find it out if he did not spend time with her.

Unfortunately, his responsibilities around the estate still waited, so he could not afford to dawdle with her as long as he would have liked. His time with her had cleared his head more than a ride on Andronicus would have. It was time to head back to the house and the ledgers he had left behind. Their steward would be waiting for him when he returned. The work to be done was great and the time he had allotted to be in Kent was short.

With genuine regret, he mounted Andronicus and set him back down the path at a trot, turning to wave good-bye to his cousin as he did. He smiled when she returned the gesture.

The horse snorted and shook his head, jangling his bridle. Richard narrowed his eyes at the stallion. Andronicus was laughing at him. "It was just a friendly gesture," he told the stallion. "We are cousins. She would expect me to be polite and show interest in her activities. Besides, I need to get to know her better. I have to make sure she knows what she is doing when it comes to running Rosings and handling her mother. Lady Catherine can be very difficult. I am simply looking out for her."

The horse craned his neck around to eye him with disbelief.

Richard sighed. "Yes, I know. I do not believe the excuses either. She is quite a woman, Andronicus. I will not deny it. But she is also my cousin. My duty toward her extends far deeper than that of a man to a woman." He looked out over the fields. "And let us face the truth. Lady Catherine would be no fonder of me as a son-in-law than Anne would have been of Darcy as a husband. An alliance between our two families is far less preferable than an alliance between Pemberley and Rosings."

He shook his head to clear his maudlin thoughts. "I must nip these thoughts in the bud before they sprout like one of Anne's roses, old boy. What do you say we go for that ride after all?"

Andronicus nickered his excitement at the prospect, and, with a chuckle, Richard turned him down another path.

The ledgers could wait a little while longer.

CHAPTER THREE

By the next day, Richard had had his fill of ledgers and meetings with the steward. The time he had spent the day before inside after returning from his ride and the hours of work that morning left him feeling as if Rosings' walls were closing in on him and holding him captive. He desperately needed a change of scenery and a breath of fresh air.

Fortunately, he had exactly the remedy for what ailed him. According to Anne's list, he needed to ride the property and inspect the tenant dwellings for any damage or necessary repairs before he finished his tenure at Rosings. He might as well do it now. With the ledgers put away and the steward dismissed to see to other duties, he took the stairs two at a time on his way to his chambers to change into his riding attire.

He whistled merrily as he strode down the hall, eager to escape Rosings' confines for a more pleasant oasis. Anne's voice, coming from the open parlor door, stopped him in his tracks.

Her voice shimmered with barely repressed annoyance. "No, Mother. I cannot listen to Mr. Collins' sermon for this Sunday with you."

"Why ever not?" demanded Lady Catherine.

Without stopping to think about it, Richard stepped into the doorway and leaned his shoulder against the frame. "Because, my dear aunt, she has already promised to go for a drive with me." He turned a wide grin on Anne, feeling magnanimous. "Are you ready to go, Cousin?"

Anne did not hesitate to take the boon he offered her. She rose gracefully. "Of course. I have only been waiting for you to finish in the study."

Lady Catherine eyed her suspiciously. "You are not dressed for a drive."

"We are headed up to change," Richard reassured his aunt. "It will not take long to make ourselves presentable enough to go for a drive."

She crossed her arms over her ample bosom and harrumphed. "Very well," she agreed begrudgingly. "I do hope you will not catch a cold, going out on a day like today."

Richard spared a glance toward the sunshine streaming through the window of the parlor. "I do not think we have to worry. The weather has held out admirably so far."

He motioned for Anne to precede him into the hall and then bid his aunt a respectful good day that did little to soften her countenance before following his cousin out.

Once they were out of earshot, Anne wound her hand through his arm and grinned up at him unrepentantly. "Your timing is impeccable, Richard."

He chuckled. "You are fortunate I came along when I did. Even I would not be so cruel as to doom you to listening to one of Mr. Collins' sermons on a weekday. The man does gone on and on interminably."

It did not take long to reach their rooms. Richard dropped his cousin at her door, then made a beeline for his own room. As soon as the door was shut behind him, he rang for Anne's pony and cart and then set about changing into suitable attire. This was a great deal less complicated for him than it was for Anne, and so he found himself waiting outside her door not a quarter hour later, ready to go.

It took almost another quarter hour for Anne to appear. She had changed out of her drab morning gown and into something more suitable for seeing and being seen in. Her hair was styled in ringlets to frame her face instead of the sleek bun she had sported half an hour earlier. Richard offered her his arm and they went downstairs, only stopping on their way out the front door so Anne could arrange a pert little poke bonnet over her curls.

It was not until Richard had handed Anne up into the cart and picked up the reins that she asked, "So, Cousin, where are we going?"

Richard grinned as he guided the pony up the drive. "I need to visit some of the tenants and see if there are any repairs to be done to their dwellings. I hope you do not mind that this is a business drive and not simply for pleasure." She really did have a lot of faith in him to go along with him without even asking where they were going. He rather liked that about her. It made him feel strong, responsible, in charge. He urged the pony to a trot.

Anne reached up to hold her bonnet securely in place as the wind threatened to cast it off her head. "I do not mind at all. I would like to visit some of our tenants and see how they are getting along. Mother does not like me going out on my own, you know, so I rarely get the opportunity to care for that aspect of the estate."

"Then it is just as well you are accompanying me," Richard said. "The task should be done more than once a year when I visit. It really needs to be done regularly, so that the tenants will feel comfortable coming to you if something happens and a repair needs to be made right away. Perhaps your mother will be more likely to allow you to visit on your own if I assure her of its necessity."

Anne shrugged. "Perhaps. However, my mother prefers to be involved with the tenants. If she knows I am going to do the rounds, then she is likely to insist upon going along."

Richard grinned at her. "Then perhaps you need to apply a little of your own logic and ask for forgiveness instead of permission."

Anne laughed. It was a surprise to have him throw her words back at her. "I can see the wisdom in your suggestion. I go out to see Mrs. Collins often enough on my own. It would be a simple matter to set off from there."

Richard nodded, "Or even after you have spent some time at your greenhouse, you might just pop in to one or two tenants before you head home. There are many opportunities, if you plan in advance."

"Indeed," she agreed. "I shall take your suggestion under advisement."

Richard turned the pony down one of the side lanes so they would not have to travel past the parsonage. Anne noted his choice with a raised brow.

"Do you not fancy dropping in on Mr. and Mrs. Collins?" she asked.

Richard snorted. "I would rather not. I would like to hope that Mr. Collins would be at Rosings by now, entertaining Aunt Catherine, but I am not taking any chances. If he were to waylay us, we will lose valuable time. Besides, I have had quite enough of inactivity for one day." He urged the pony to a faster clip.

Anne eyed him from the corner of her eye. "I can see that. I do not suppose you would take pity on my bonnet and refrain from being quite so active?"

Richard let his mouth quirk up ruefully and slowed the pony back to a more reasonable clip. "I do apologize. I am afraid those ledgers have taken more of a toll on me than I realized."

Anne's mouth twitched with amusement. "It is rare that I hear a man blame ledgers for driving him to escape the house. I thought it was only manipulative mamas trying to push their daughters on a man that could claim that honor."

He laughed and shook his head. "I fear I am not well-suited to either manipulative mamas or being trapped indoors. Those mamas have many better options than me for their daughters."

Anne stole a glance at him. "I find that difficult to believe."

Richard's mouth twisted wryly. "Believe it. Second sons are not nearly as enticing for a woman of the Ton as the many lords and dukes that grace the halls of London. There are enough of them that no woman need ever look twice at me."

"They may not need to look twice, but they most assuredly do," Anne told him bluntly. "Why, even Darcy has been known to tease you for the attention you garner among the Ton! You are a genuine, jovial fellow, and well-liked. Even Elizabeth can attest to that. She felt comfortable enough with you to tease Darcy about his dreadful behavior in front of you."

"That is true enough," Richard answered, slowing the cart as they came upon a difficult stream crossing. This route was not without its challenges, but he deemed them to be well worth the effort not to have to deal with the annoying Mr. Collins. "I cannot say I have not made a great many friends from my time on the marriage mart. Yet, I have never had the occasion to propose marriage as well."

Anne had no response for that comment, which was just as well, as they were entering the stream. The streambed was rocky and unlevel, and it was a crossing Anne would never have dared to try on her own. Even Richard's impressive driving skills were going to be put to the test. Anne clutched the side of the rig, her knuckles white. "Are you sure this is the best idea? It is not too late to turn around and go back by the way of the parsonage. Surely Mr. Collins would have departed for his meeting with my mother by now."

Richard's hands tightened around the reins. "There is no sense turning around now. We have already come this far. It would be a waste of time to go back around the other way."

She flashed him an irritated glance, but held her tongue. She knew a stubborn man when she saw one. There was nothing she could say or do that would change his mind. All she could do was pray for the best and hold on for dear life as the cart rattled into the water.

It was not a particularly deep stream, for which Anne found herself thankful. The water only rose up the wheels about six inches in the deepest parts. It was the uneven terrain that made the crossing so tricky. Anne gritted her teeth against the jarring ride. The unsprung cart was not made for comfort on the best of drives, and this could hardly qualify as that.

Richard guided the pony with steady hands, choosing his path carefully. Anne appreciated his diligence, but she could not help but think they would have been better off going the long way around. Not that she could change that now.

She breathed a sigh of relief as the cart started up the other side of the stream bank, the crossing safely behind them.

Richard turned to her with a grin. "See, that was not so bad, was it? We made it through just fine."

Anne opened her mouth to voice her begrudging agreement at the same time that the cart dropped into a large hole. The right wheel splintered, leaving Anne's side of the cart dipping dangerously. Anne let out a squeak and grabbed a fistful of Richard's jacket to steady herself as he quickly reined in the pony.

He scooted over on the seat, tugging Anne with him until she was no longer hanging precariously over the broken wheel. He offered her a chagrined smile. "I may have spoken too soon."

A little breathless- whether from fright at the sudden jolt or Richard's touch, she could not say- she responded, "I should say so."

Richard released her, leaving her feeling just the slightest bit bereft, and more than a little confused by her strange reaction. "I shall just go inspect the damage and see what can be done about it."

He hopped down from the cart and went around the front, laying a soothing hand on the pony's withers as he crouched to inspect the damage.

It was quite beyond repair. Or at least, it was beyond the scope of repairs Richard could make in their current situation. He would have to leave that job for the professionals. He sighed and glanced up at Anne, who was peering over the side of the cart at him with concern. "We are going to have to walk back."

"Let me see." She scooted a little closer so she could see the damage for herself, the side of the cart dipping and swaying under her weight.

Richard reached up a hand to steady her. "Do not come any farther," he warned. "I do not want this side of the cart to collapse and cause you to fall. It is a long walk back to Rosings and that pony will not carry both of us."

She glanced at the pony, who was craning its neck around to watch Richard anxiously. The poor animal was badly shaken by their accident. She did not trust it not to run away with her if she was up on its back. She turned her attention back to Richard, who was frowning at the wheel. "What are we going to do?"

He sighed. "I suppose the only thing we can do. We walk back to Rosings and send someone back to fetch the cart so it can be repaired." He glanced at her, a wry smile tilting his lips. "I am afraid our visit to the tenants shall have to be postponed for another day."

Anne accepted the reasonableness of their change in plans even as she acknowledged her frustration at having to put off the excursion to another day. If she was not able to take advantage of this opportunity to go with Richard, it was unlikely she would be able to accompany him if he decided to go out again on another day. And while she accepted and appreciated his proposal that she make opportunities to visit her tenants, it would have gone a long way toward smoothing her introduction to the task if she had been able to accompany him. There would be no opportunity now to learn from his example. What questions did one ask? How did she walk the line between wishing to provide for the needs of her tenants and allowing them a measure of pride and self-sufficiency? Anne had experienced the process at Lady Catherine's side, but she had a feeling the entire thing would go much more smoothly under Richard's tutelage. Now she would likely never have the opportunity to learn from him.

She allowed Richard to help her out of the cart, his hands around her waist sending tendrils of awareness through her. She had been helped out of a carriage many times over the years, but no other man's touch had ever set her so off balance. She hung on to his lapels a few moments longer than necessary, just to make sure she had her footing. The broad expanse of his chest was a firm support under her palms. Richard did not seem to be in a hurry to release her, biding his time until she stepped away on her own.

She did not dare to look up as she passed by him to grab the pony's bridle and murmur consolingly in its ears. Her pink cheeks would have given away her discomfort and acute awareness of him and she could not afford to let him peek under her carefully polished armor.

She was already too comfortable with him, too at home. It was more than the fact that they were cousins and had associated for most of their lives. Richard was different than she remembered him. He seemed to *see* her now. She could not hide from him. And most of the time she did not want to. But right now, when her own thoughts and feelings toward him were so confusing, she did not dare let on to the turn they had taken.

Richard joined her at the pony's head. "I suppose we should unharness him and lead him back. It would hardly be fair to expect him to stand here and wait for a rescue party to come back."

"No. That would be unnecessarily distressing, indeed. I would hate to think of the poor dear alone out here and know we had abandoned him," Anne agreed.

"It should be an easy enough job," Richard said, then set about unhitching the pony with deft fingers. Considering that it was not his job, he certainly seemed to know what he was doing. Then again, he had spent most of his adult life in the military. He had probably been called upon to do the task more than once in his lifetime. In a matter of minutes, the job was done.

He took the bridle from her hands before the pony could take the bit between its teeth and run and turned the animal in a wide arc, leading it out of its tracings. Only then did he seem to consider that they were going to have to go back the way they had come, which meant traversing the stream they had just crossed.

Richard grimaced and Anne hid her smile. Right about now he was really regretting his decision to ignore her qualms. As tempting as it was to rub it in, she resisted the urge.

Richard looked at the water, then at her, the pony, and back at the water. He heaved a long-suffering sigh. "Nothing can be simple, can it?"

She giggled, a surprisingly girlish sound for one who had long passed into the realm of spinsterhood. "It never is."

He studied her mournfully. "I do not suppose you would know of another way around?"

She shook her head, fighting a smile. "Not unless you want to walk all the way around the estate and return by way of the parsonage. However, that would be quite out of the way."

He heaved another sigh. "Then I suppose there is no other way but through the stream."

She bit her bottom lip and nodded.

"Very well," he said. "Let me help you on to the pony. There is no reason for us both to get wet, and I cannot run the risk of you catching your death of a cold walking back with wet skirts."

Anne's mouth twitched. "You do not think my mother would be impressed if I came back with my hem six inches deep in mud?"

He cast her a long-suffering glance. She might be enjoying his discomfort, but he was not amused. Still, she could not resist the urge to tease him. She said with mock horror, "What will my mother say when she sees the state of your trousers? Surely no gentleman would ever so despoil the gates of Rosings!"

His mouth turned up begrudgingly. "You are going to get us both in trouble."

She grinned unrepentantly and fluttered her eyelashes coyly. "Surely not. I am but a gentlewoman, forced into demure subservience. I would not dare to suggest I might know better than a gentleman such as yourself. I simply could not be to blame for a situation such as this."

He laughed outright this time. "Come on, Anne. Up with you before I take up the gentlemanly notion to toss you in the stream and see how well you fare on your own."

A huge grin splitting her face, she did as she was told, and allowed Richard to help her on to the pony's back.

Without the benefit of a saddle, or a riding habit, for that matter, it was a slippery proposition and Anne knew it would only become even more so once they entered the water and the pony had to pick its footing. She wrapped her hands in the pony's mane and held on for dear life, trying to ignore how unseemly it was that her ankles and calves peeked out from under her hemline.

Richard peered up at her, noting her precarious situation, but he was too much of a gentleman to comment on her indecorous position. "It is not very far. Do you think you can hang on until we are across?"

Anne nodded, thanking God for small favors and Richard's averted eyes. "I believe so."

He did not look convinced. He held the long reins coiled in one hand while supporting her with the other. His hand against the small of her back was infinitely distracting, his strong fingers branding their imprint into her skin through the material of her dress and chemise and making it difficult to concentrate on keeping her seat.

She felt herself sliding and tightened her knees against the pony at the same time Richard caught her around the waist, halting her fall. With Richard torn between holding on to the pony's reins and keeping her from falling, Anne ended up wedged between the pony and his body, the full length of his torso pressed up against her uncomfortably.

Heat flashed through her, embarrassment and discomfort and something else searing her- something far more powerful that she did not dare to name. Her lungs felt tight and hot, too scorched to draw in breath and yet she did not think all the air in the world could set her heart back to its normal rhythm. She giggled, her uneasiness showing itself as nerves. "Well, this is awkward."

Richard's mouth twisted up wryly. "You have an uncanny knack for understatement." He hunched up the shoulder closer to her. "Put your hand on my shoulder and see if you can push yourself back into place."

She obeyed, guilt crashing through her when he grunted under the strain of her weight as she righted herself. She peered down at him anxiously, her nerves forgotten. "Have I hurt you?"

His mouth turned up. "Never fear, Cousin. Your slight weight is not enough to break me."

She could not help grinning at him. "What a chauvinistic statement to make. Have I offended your delicate male sensibilities again?"

He roared with laughter, having to admit that he had come off sounding that way. "I do apologize, Anne. That was not my intention. Let us get across this and get you back on solid ground, shall we?"

With the tension between them broken, and Anne more securely situated, they approached the stream.

Very carefully, they crossed. Richard chose each step with caution, planting his feet firmly and grimacing as the icy water penetrated his boots and pants. Anne could not help cringing sympathetically when a stone came loose under his foot, causing him to stumble and go down to one knee in the water. He picked himself back up and carried on, but she knew his legs had to be numb from the cold by the time they safely reached the other side.

She slid from the pony's back as soon as he drew the animal to a halt, rearranging her skirts modestly back around her ankles with a sigh of relief.

Richard glanced back at her to reassure himself she had made it across unharmed and dry and was surprised to see her already on the ground, studying him seriously. He suppressed a shiver as she ran her gaze over his body from head to toe. He tried to tell himself it was from the frigid water, but it was not, not really.

When she looked at him like that, he could almost imagine she could see right through him to the man he was underneath, the man who wanted so much more out of life than the hand he had been dealt as a second son.

But that was impossible. No one knew what dreams and hopes secretly lurked there. He had been careful to tamp down those forbidden desires for hearth and home. They did not belong to him and he did well to remember it. Most of the time, at least. When Anne was looking at him like that, though, like she cared about him and his welfare, it was hard to remember he could not have those things.

He turned his gaze away, ostensibly to check over the pony, but really to give himself a few moments to regain his composure and make sure his defenses were still in place.

Anne joined him at the pony's head, stroking its nose and murmuring into its ears about what a fine animal it was. He smiled and shook his head at her compliments. "You shall have no one to blame but yourself if he gets a big head like Andronicus."

She peeked up at him from under her lashes, smiling. "If my pony turns out to be half as talented as your stallion, he shall be deserving of a big head. Andronicus is a fine specimen, much like his owner."

Richard ducked his head to avoid her appraising eyes. "Ho, you do not want me to get a big head as well, now, do you?" He chuckled in an attempt to brush off her compliment and clucked to the pony to get it moving again.

They plodded off at an easy pace, leaving Anne to catch up with them. She frowned at him as she came alongside, but chose to keep her thoughts to herself, for which Richard was grateful. He was not sure he cared to know what was running through her mind, not when it just might set his whole world to spinning.

"Andronicus and you seem to have a very special relationship," Anne commented after a lengthy pause, turning the topic to a less troublesome subject.

Richard smiled, glad for the welcome change in topic and pleased with her choice. His mount was a subject dear to his heart, and very few people recognized the bond they shared. "We do. Andronicus and I have been through a lot together, more than most humans relationships see in a lifetime. He may be just an old war horse, but he is *my* war horse."

Anne nodded, her gaze drinking in the intensity of his expression. That horse meant a lot to him. "You speak of him almost as a person."

Richard's mouth turned up. "I suppose I do. He practically is one to me, for all intents and purposes. I suspect I talk more to that horse than I do to any one person. He has been a good friend over the years, better to me than any other comrade."

Perhaps a safer friend, too, given the dangers of war. He risked less pain and heartbreak by not getting attached to the men that might soon fall by his side. Too many had done just that. Yet, somehow, he and Andronicus had made it through. He was grateful for that blessing.

He preferred not to talk about such a difficult subject, so he transferred his gaze to the pretty young woman walking beside him. "What about you? Have you ever had a pet?"

She glanced up at him, her warm gaze making his breath hitch in his chest. He rubbed at the spot absentmindedly.

"Oh, not in the way you have Andronicus. Indeed, my mother has always strongly asserted that having animals in the house is bad for one's health, especially mine. If I wanted to play with one of the puppies or kittens I had to sneak out to the stables and hope one of the servants would not see me and tell Mother."

He could see the wistfulness in her gaze. "I have always thought having a pet to be a vital part of one's upbringing," he stated firmly. "They can be quite beneficial for children, especially if one does not have siblings to play with. At home growing up there was always a dog or three running around."

She smiled softly. "It would have been pleasant to have a pet to keep me company, especially during the days I was trapped inside because of illness and Mother's overprotective nature. Those were some lonely times." She glanced at him and felt compelled to add, "Thankfully they are behind me now." She did not want him to think she was trying to fill that empty void with his company.

She was content with her life, filling what had previously been lonely days with hard work and cheerful diligence. There was much to occupy her time with on the estate, especially now that Mrs. Collins had moved into the parsonage. The arrival of her new son or daughter would only bring more joy and life to Rosings.

Richard turned to look at her, cocking his head curiously. "What is behind you? Your bouts of illness or lonely days?"

Anne ducked her head and concentrated on picking out a path through the gravel. "Both."

She did not look up, but she could tell that Richard watched her as they walked.

"I imagine Mrs. Collins' arrival alleviated some of your boredom and loneliness," he mused quietly. "Still, it cannot be easy to spend so much time at Rosings with only your mother for company."

Anne forced a smile to her lips and looked up to meet his gaze. "You forget I have your visits to look forward to once a year. Besides, Rosings is a fine estate. There is much to do here."

"Uh huh," Richard murmured, looking dubious.

Anne knew she sounded too defensive, but she could not take the words back now. The truth was, she did live a fine life. She knew many a young woman would covet the position she held.

And while she had her fair share of loneliness and longing for a different life, she had come to grips with the life she had. There was much to be thankful for, and Anne knew how to count her blessings. She was fortunate just to be here. There had been a time, as a child, when that future had not been so certain.

She softened her tone, letting her sincerity shine in her eyes as she told Richard, "I have a fine life, with no reason to complain. Truly. There was a time I might not have been able to say that, but it is the truth now. And I truly do value your visits to Rosings. They are the highlight of my year." Her smile widened. "This year promises to be much of the same."

He chuckled. "I am glad to know that someone here values my company."

"Not just your company," she reminded him. "Your assistance about the estate is very welcome as well."

He shrugged. "You do not need me for that. You have that job well in hand."

She fought a smile at his confidence, for she knew very well it had been hard won. He had not been so confident only a day ago when he had sought her out at the greenhouse. "Thank you. Still, I prefer to have a helping hand. Your assistance is certainly appreciated. I know my steward feels the same way. While we may be capable of handling the estate on our own, another set of hands makes the load lighter for us all."

Richard chuckled. "That sounds like a philosophy Mr. Collins would espouse and Lady Catherine would eschew."

Anne laughed. "It does. Perhaps I should bring it up the next time I am cornered in a room with both of them and see what mayhem might ensue."

He shook his head. "No, for Mr. Collins would promptly eschew any opinions he might hold in favor of Lady Catherine's opinion, and then there would be no reasoning with your mother."

Anne grinned, acknowledging the truth in his statement. Up ahead, the woods were starting to thin to pastureland. She could just make out the beginnings of the stone fence line that partitioned off the field where the flocks grazed from the drive to Rosings. Wooden gates in the walls gave the shepherds access to the roads to move their flocks when necessary.

She pointed out the change in scenery. "Once we pass the pastures, it will not be much longer before we reach the house."

Richard grinned. "You sound anxious to be rid of me."

She laughed. "Never. However, I am anxious to get out of these shoes. I did not expect to be walking quite so much and I am afraid I did not wear the proper footgear."

She held up a foot so he could see the thinness of her sole. He grimaced. "You must be able to feel every pebble in the road with those things."

"Very nearly," she agreed. "Still, it is preferable to trying to maintain my dignity on horseback." She gestured to her light gown. "I am afraid this dress was no more made for riding bareback than my shoes were made for walking."

Richard's mind flashed back to the pretty picture she painted riding bareback. He could not help but think she had looked beautiful, wild and free, unfettered by the usual restraints of society and her mother's expectations. However, he could very well imagine Lady Catherine's response to such an escapade. Her hems had been half up her calves, her dainty ankles exposed, and her grip precarious. Those ankles, though…Richard had done his best not to stare, to concentrate on the pony, and not the woman gracing its back. It had been difficult. He could admit he would not have wanted any other man seeing her in such a state.

Even he should not have seen her in that state, but it could not be helped. He tried to justify it. They were cousins, after all. It was not as if the normal statures of society applied to them. However, the feelings that swirled in him in her company were decidedly not cousinly. Richard pushed those thoughts to the back of his mind.

He needed to concentrate on getting Anne home safe and sound, not on how enchanting he found the sight of her ankles.

They had reached the beginning of the stone wall by now and were just passing one of the wooden gates. "You are not the only one who was not prep-"

A blur of white fur and teeth streaking out from under the gate cut him off. The dog made straight for them, barking and growling and baring his teeth with displeasure. Without conscious thought, Richard grabbed Anne by the waist and swung her behind him, ignoring her yelp of surprise. "Stay behind me."

The dog skidded to a halt only a few feet from them, his low growl threatening menace.

"No problem there," she muttered.

Richard eyed the dog. It was one of the shaggy giants the shepherds used to help herd their sheep. He had heard that sometimes the animals were a mite overprotective when it came to their charges, but he had never experienced it for himself. This one seemed to think they were a threat of some sort, although that was far from the case.

"It is alright, fellow," Richard said soothingly. "We have no wish to harm your flock. We just want to continue on our way in peace." He tried to ignore the pony skittering on the end of the reins he held, eyes rolling in fear. He could not calm both animals at once, but he did tighten his grip on the reins. It would certainly not help matters if the pony got away from him and bolted for the house. The last thing he wanted was to bring Lady Catherine in all her glory down upon them.

Anne peeked over his shoulder and whispered, "Do you think he is going to attack us?"

"Not if I can prevent it," Richard whispered back. He tried to ignore the puff of her breath against his ear and the shiver it sent running down his spine. That woman was going to be the death of him if she did not do as he had told her and stay back. There was no way he could handle the pony, the dog, and her, all at the same time.

She was a distraction, plain and simple. And one he definitely did not need at the moment.

The dog chose that moment to let out another rumbling growl and take one menacing step forward. Anne squealed and buried her face between Richard's shoulder blades, effectively ending any conversation between them.

Richard was torn between the desire to comfort her and the desire to protect her from the vicious dog. The urge to gather her in his arms was overpowering, but he did not dare to turn his back.

A shrill whistle split the air, bringing both his head and the dog's up. Over the fence, deep in the pasture, Richard could just make out the figure of the shepherd, calling his dog.

He looked back at the white menace still threatening them. The dog looked decidedly torn between heeding his master's call and protecting the flock from intruders.

The whistle rent the air again, and this time, the dog let out one last indignant bark and then turned tail and ran to join his master, disappearing under the gate as quickly as he had appeared.

Richard let out a sigh of relief and gave into the urge he had been battling. He turned around and pulled Anne into his arms, reassuring himself that she was safe and unharmed. He bent his head to press his temple against hers and inhale the sweet scent of her hair. "What a string of disasters this trip has been," he said with a mirthless chuckle.

She patted his chest. "It has certainly been memorable, I will give you that."

The breeze shifted, blowing one tantalizing curl across his face and making him wish this moment could last forever.

Anne was more than he ever would have expected. She was different than any other woman that he had ever met. Indeed, she was a completely different person than the persona she presented in the drawing room with her mother. He was grateful for the opportunity to get to know her this trip. Really know her. And to see all the wonderful facets of her personality that made her the complex, forthright, endearing woman she was.

She was not intimidated by him. Nor was she disrespectful. She had a knack for honesty that made her say things the way they were unapologetically. That was enough to brand her as a rare find in his book.

Unfortunately, she did not belong to him. Reluctantly, he stepped back, dropping his arms from around her, and cleared his throat. "I suppose we should be getting back before any other danger decides to befall us."

"I had no idea Rosings was so fraught with hazards. Perhaps my mother was wise to keep me near the house in my childhood." Anne grinned at him, seemingly unfazed by his embrace. He wished he could say the same. Holding her in his arms had left him decidedly confused.

No other woman had ever produced the same reaction in him. Then again, he had never dared to take such liberties with a woman before. If they were not related, he would never have done so with Anne, despite the circumstances. Perhaps that accounted for the strange uptick in his heart rate.

Yes, that was most assuredly the reason for his disquiet. He tried to dismiss his traitorous heart with the logical explanation, but doubt lingered and he was forced to admit that he was lying to himself. As much as he would have liked to explain away his lingering awareness of her and the ache in his soul that holding her in his arms had soothed, there was no logical explanation.

He very much feared that the explanation for that was in the region of his heart, where logic had no jurisdiction.

So, instead of trying to wrangle his heart into submission, he offered Anne his free arm. "Shall we?"

She took it, smiling widely. "We shall." The sun chose that moment to peek out from the clouds, bathing her in light and glory. She raised her face to its warmth, holding her bonnet to her head with one hand. "I daresay it has turned into a lovely day for a drive after all, despite my mother's warnings."

Richard swallowed hard, his mouth too dry to speak. Why, oh why, did she have to be so appealing with the sunshine highlighting her curls and bringing color to her cheeks? Her radiance was captivating. He could not look away, even though he tried.

Lord knows, he tried. He even reminded himself of the pony that continually tugged on its lead. But nothing worked.

She turned that smile on him and he forgot everything else. His purpose for being at Rosings, her mother's summons, the goal of their drive. All of it. It was gone, out of his head.

All he knew was that she was beautiful, and she was here with him. She could have been strolling down this lane on any other gentleman's arm. But she was not. She was with him, and by her own choice. There could be no other greater blessing, despite the wrong turns their path had already taken that day.

Richard felt his own smile blossoming in response to hers. "You are absolutely right. This is a wonderful day for a stroll. Let us make the most of it, shall we?"

Her smile was all the answer he needed.

66

CHAPTER FOUR

A few days later, the weather was dreary and wet, as was often the case in Kent in the spring. Anne turned from the window, where she had been gazing longingly at the path that led to her greenhouse, and went to sit at the little desk in her sitting room. Her steward had returned the latest ledger to her only that morning, with Fitzwilliam's thanks.

Although she had not expected Richard to deliver the volume personally when he finished reviewing it, she had been disappointed when it was not him on the other side of her door.

She had not seen Fitzwilliam in the intervening days since he had tried to take her to see the tenants. She understood he was busy. The list she had drafted for him demanded that of him. Still, after those first few days, she had rather hoped that he would become a regular feature of her day-to-day life at Rosings. It would have been a pleasant change.

With a sigh, she dropped her chin into her palm and turned the pages until she found the empty column where the next entry went. She ran her finger over the notes he had made in the margins, double checking her figures. She knew there was nothing wrong with the numbers she had calculated, but it was still nice to know he had not found any discrepancies. Then, at the bottom of the page, her finger came to rest on a single line he had scrawled. *All looks well here. Good job.*

She smiled at the little note, knowing it had been written just for her. It was kind of him to give her that little acknowledgment, a pat on the back for a job well done. She knew he would not have done the same had it simply been her steward on the other end of the page, or any other man for that matter. No, he had done it to show his approval of her hard work, a sort of apology for ever doubting she might not have been able to handle the job.

For she knew he must have doubted. He would not have been out for a ride on Andronicus and stumbled upon her at the greenhouse if he had not. She knew her cousin well enough after watching him all these years that she knew his tells. He had been bothered when he rode up. His very choice of riding trail told her that. He was not out for a leisurely ride or to inspect the estate. He had been looking for a run and Andronicus had been prepared to give him one.

She smiled softly to herself. That horse was just as fond of him as he was of it. They had been together for a long time and shared experiences she could only imagine. She found herself wishing for the same sort of relationship with her cousin that he shared with his mount. From the conversations she had overheard between the two, it was obvious he did not hesitate to really share his thoughts and feelings with the stallion. He had yet to extend her the same courtesy, as much as she had hinted that it would be welcome.

She traced a finger over his words. *Good job*. She *was* doing a good job, but she dearly wished she did not have to do the job on her own. What a pleasure it would be to share the burden with someone else on a more permanent basis! What joy would it bring to her dull life to have someone to work side by side with?

The door to the hall swung open without preamble, startling her half out of her seat. Her mother came marching in, followed closely by her lady's maid. "Anne, you must arise at once!" She did a double take at the sight of Anne at her desk. "Oh, good. You are up. We are having guests to dinner tonight and I must insist upon you looking your best."

She waved the uncertain young maid forward imperiously. "Hansen here will see to your wardrobe and hair. I have informed her of all the details." She frowned at Anne suddenly, then barked, "And see to it that you put some color into those cheeks. You are looking gray around the gills this morning. I will not have you becoming ill tonight!"

Anne sank back into her chair, deciding it was ludicrous to try to dissuade her mother when she was on one of her rampages. Whenever she got like this, she would be satisfied with nothing less than complete obedience. She could, however, try to extract some more information to make sense of the situation. "Why is this dinner party so important, Mother? Mr. and Mrs. Collins have often seen me when I was at less than my best." Did this insistence on her appearance have something to do with Richard? Her heart beat a little faster at the prospect.

Lady Catherine sniffed and dropped unceremoniously into one of the armchairs by the hearth. Anne eyed her dolefully and hoped that her posture did not mean her mother meant to oversee the process of getting her ready.

"You do not need to act so pretentious, chit. I told you earlier in the week I was planning on throwing a dinner party. Mr. and Mrs. Collins are only a supplement to our family party when we should desire some company. Since your cousin Richard is here, I thought he might enjoy some male company of his own age. Those young men do like to linger over their port and without Darcy around to count on, we needed someone else. We must keep the numbers even, you know."

Anne found this rambling to be rather difficult to follow, especially the part about keeping the numbers even. Had her mother invited someone else to dinner? She did not think her mother had any desire to see anyone outside of her own circle of influence in Kent, and Mr. Collins was the nearest thing to a young man they had here.

She tamped down her impatience. "Are we expecting other guests?" She quickly ran over the dinner menu in her head, wondering what could be stretched and what would have to be abandoned to feed more guests. Her mother's spontaneous decisions often derailed her budget, but the cook was excellent at making something out of nothing. She was fortunate to be blessed with such talented help, which she was sure to tell them often.

Her mother huffed. "Of course we are expecting other guests!"

Anne fought the urge to roll her eyes and remained silent as she waited for her mother to explain.

"When my dear sister confirmed that Richard would be coming, I wrote to my old friend Mrs. Bellingham. She is getting rather up in years, you know, and sicklier every day-"

Anne thought, rather ironically, that Mrs. Bellingham was only a year or two older than her mother, a fact her mother liked to conveniently forget.

"-I have told her over and over again that she must walk about and find something with which to fill her time. I have extolled the many virtues of our Mr. Collins and that if she really wants to feel well she must take a firm hold on her parish and actively participate in their care. I am sure if she took an interest in them, and advised her pastor much as I advise Mr. Collins, she would be feeling much more the thing. Yet, she continues to hem and haw on the subject, claiming her knowledge is not as encompassing as mine is and she would never dare to suggest she knows more than the preacher. I flatter myself to think she is quite right. There are few that could surpass my understanding on any subject. Still, I know her dearest wish before she dies is to see her son, Mr. Gyles Bellingham, married with a family of his own."

The swift change of topic took Anne by surprise. One moment they were talking about old age and the next marriage and babies. However, her mother was not done speaking. Anne closed her gaping mouth and tried to appear attentive.

"When I found out Richard was coming, I knew I simply must invite Mr. Bellingham to come to Rosings as well. I do believe they will get along famously. Gyles is just the right sort of gentleman." She ticked off his accomplishments on her fingers. "He owns an estate in Yorkshire. He comes from an old, landed family. He does not gamble and he drinks reasonably. Oh, and I am told he is quite handsome." She paused and smiled generously. "He is just the sort of man I should like as a son-in-law."

Anne very nearly fell out of her seat. "A son-in-law!" she sputtered. "Surely not, Mother!"

Her mother peered at her as if she had grown two heads. "Why ever not? Am I not allowed to have grandchildren in my old age? Must I go to the grave with no legacy?"

Anne fought to catch the breath that had suddenly deflated her lungs and floundered for some sort of a response. "I do not know what to say."

Lady Catherine smiled smugly. "You need not say anything at all. I know what is best for you, daughter, and I am determined that Gyles Bellingham is just the thing. You will look your best for him tonight, and when he offers to take you driving in the coming days, you will accept. I expect you to give him your full attention. Opportunities like this do not come along every day. You must snag his attention while he is here. Hansen will see to it that you start out right by looking your best tonight." She pushed herself out of the armchair with no little exertion. "Now, I must see to Mr. Bellingham's accommodations. We must make sure our guest feels quite at home." She frowned. "I do wish the housekeeper had not given Richard the chamber in the tower, but I suppose that cannot be helped now. It would most likely be considered rude to ask him to move. We shall just have to put Gyles in Richard's usual room."

She was already calling for the housekeeper as she exited Anne's apartment, her sharp voice ringing in the hall.

Anne grimaced. What a mess this was turning out to be. She rubbed at her forehead and then lifted her gaze to find Hansen regarding her sympathetically. She was not the only one her mother had put into an awkward position.

If she and Hansen were feeling put out upon, she could only imagine what Mr. Bellingham was feeling. Most likely the young man was only trying to make his mother and hers happy, and had no more interest in her than a bee had in a buzzard.

She sighed and asked, "What gown did my mother insist upon, Hansen?"

The maid stepped forward. "The peach silk."

Anne wrinkled her nose. Her father had bought that gown for her before he died, a gift meant for her London debut. It was dreadfully out of style now. "I do not suppose there is much we can do to make it over with the time we have."

"I believe we may be able to make enough adjustments to bring it into the modern age if we begin work right away. I had a chat with some of the girls below stairs and we came up with a plan. Shall I show you?"

Anne nodded, relieved. "Yes. Please do."

Hansen went to retrieve the gown, giving Anne a moment to herself. She had a lot of faith in the women she employed, but even she did not expect them to work miracles.

Hansen brought out the dress, holding it up for her to inspect. Anne caught her breath at the bittersweet memories that welled up at the sight of it. Her father had been so proud of this dress and her in it. She would be the belle of the ball, he told her, a veritable princess. And she had believed him.

What girl did not believe her father when he said something was so? She reached out to finger the peach silk with a fond smile. He had told her the color would bring out the pink in her cheeks and some fine gentleman would swirl her around the dance floor before begging for her hand in marriage.

She dropped her hand and took a step back. Life had not turned out to be the fairytale her father had made it out to be.

A short while after, her father had died, leaving her with a distraught mother who had never really recovered. The gown had been relegated to the back of her wardrobe and forgotten about for years. Even after the period of mourning had passed, Anne had continued to wear the drab, dull colors her mother chose for her.

For what purpose had her mother insisted on bringing this gown back out again? It would do no good to bring back the past. There was no going back to those happier times.

Still, she could not ignore her mother's wishes. She asked Hansen, "What do you plan to do?"

The maid detailed the plan they had to bring the voluminous dress down to the more current styles. Anne nodded, agreeing with the suggestions she made. The gown would not compare to the fashionable dresses worn in London, but it would be well within what would be expected in the country.

With her approval for the changes, the maid departed, gown in hand, and Anne was left to finish making the latest entries in the ledger. It should have been a fairly simple task that only took a quarter of an hour, but she found it surprisingly difficult to concentrate after her mother's interruption.

Did her mother really expect her to marry Gyles Bellingham? She did not even know the man. She had only briefly met his mother on one occasion before.

She had heard of him, of course, for her mother dearly loved to share the letters she received from her friends and the long responses filled with advice she sent in return. She had to admit, from what she knew of him there was little to find fault with. Still, she could hardly expect the missives of his mother to be without bias. Perhaps Richard would be able to tell her more about the man before he arrived. Surely, if her mother thought Gyles would serve as an excellent companion for him the two men must have met in the past. She trusted his opinion. If he spoke highly of the other man she would have to give him a chance to prove himself, no matter how unlikely she thought a romance between them would be.

She rose and paced to the window, looking out at the gray clouds. Where would Richard be? She had not thought to ask the steward when he dropped off the ledgers, but surely on a day as dismal as this one he would be indoors.

Movement in the stable yard caught her eye as a groom dashed across the courtyard. She grinned. Of course! She knew precisely where Richard would be on a day like this, when the weather prevented him from taking a morning ride about the property.

Her steps light, she crossed the room to the door and stepped into the hallway, the ledger on her desk all but forgotten.

*****

Fitzwilliam inspected the bridle he held, then worked a little more wax into the leather. The straw bale he sat on in his stallion's stall was prickly, but at least it was dry, unlike most of the estate. Andronicus nudged his shoulder with his nose and whickered entreatingly but Fitzwilliam did not look up from his task. "I know, old chap. The weather cannot be helped today. You will just have to be patient."

The horse snorted and stepped away to hang his head over the divider into the aisle.

Richard chuckled. "You can ignore me all you want, but the decision will still be the same. We are not going out in the rain."

Andronicus just sidestepped to present Richard with his rear, and emphasized his displeasure with a swish of his tail. Out of sight in the aisle, someone giggled. That brought Richard's head up. "Who goes there?"

A petite hand reached over the stall wall to pat Andronicus' nose sympathetically. "He is grumpy today, is he not, Andronicus?" A moment later a dark head popped into sight and Anne grinned down at him. "You need not be so curt, Colonel. I mean no harm. Shall I stand down?"

Richard smiled reluctantly at her teasing. "I apologize. Old habits die hard."

She accepted his apology with a nod. "It is of no matter. I wished to speak to you. May I come in?"

Richard looked around the stall, clean thanks to his recent handiwork, and could not conceal a rueful chuckle. She was treating his horse's stall as if it was the drawing room in a fine manor house. "I do not see why not, as long as you do not mind a hay bale for a seat. I regret I cannot offer you anything finer unless you prefer to have this conversation in the house."

"A hay bale is fine," she assured him, opening the stall door and slipping past Andronicus.

The horse craned his head around to watch her perch on the hay bale, primly smoothing her skirts over her knees. He eyed his owner speculatively. Richard knew exactly what the big stallion was thinking. Anne's presence might have boosted his mood, but it did not mean he was going to change his mind. With narrowed eyes, Richard shook his head at the animal. Andronicus snorted and stomped his foot, then went back to watching the activity down at the other end of the aisle as one of the grooms brought Anne's pony out of its stall for a brushing.

Fitzwilliam waited until she had settled herself, and then, when nothing else was forthcoming, asked, "So what did you wish to speak to me about?"

She fidgeted with her sleeve, a delaying tactic he found strange for her to use. In all their interactions, she had never hesitated to speak her mind. What would change that now?

Finally, she heaved a sigh and dropped her hands behind her, leaning back on them to brace herself against the hay bale. "I wanted to talk to you about Gyles Bellingham."

Confused, he repeated, "Gyles Bellingham?"

She nodded. "You know him, do you not?"

"Yes," he admitted. "Albeit not well. We are barely acquainted. I really know more *of* him than I *know* him. Why would you wish to know about him?"

She rubbed at her forehead and avoided his eyes. "Mother has invited him to stay with us while you are here."

His suspicions were immediately sparked, especially when she would not meet his eyes, but he managed to keep his face stoic and innocent. Lady Catherine did nothing without a motive. Even Anne knew that. She was hiding something from him. It only remained to be seen how long she would attempt to keep her secret and for what purpose.

Nonchalantly, he said, "That is interesting. I did not know your mother had any connections to the Bellingham family."

She bit her bottom lip, another telling sign she was withholding information from him. "She has often corresponded with his mother. They were childhood friends before they married."

Richard studied her, his eyes astute. She was sure he could see right through her unstudied visage. She was nearly ready to abandon the pretense and spill her fears and worries, but the truth was too embarrassing to admit to so easily.

"Mother seemed to think you would appreciate another male presence around the dinner table." That much was certainly true, even if it was not her mother's real motive.

He nodded, but she did not think he was really agreeing with her. That nod was one of confirmation. "So she was looking for a way to bring another man into the house and I was a convenient excuse."

Her face flamed, telling him he had lit upon the true reason for Lady Catherine's guise. "It seems so."

Richard frowned heavily. He did not like to be manipulated, not even inadvertently, but he had to remember Anne was not the real culprit here. Her mother had used her just as assuredly as Lady Catherine had used him to get her way. He refocused on her. He still did not have the complete story. "Why does she want another man in the house?" He had his suspicions, but he wanted to hear it from her mouth.

He did not think she could get any pinker, but apparently he was wrong. The flush in her cheeks crept into her hairline. "I am not sure I can fully explain my mother's reasoning."

Now that was an interesting response. He cocked his head. "Whatever do you mean by that?"

She looked away, then back again, meeting his eyes reluctantly. "She has decided she likes the idea of Gyles Bellingham as a son-in-law."

Richard was momentarily stunned into silence. Then he burst out laughing. "She has never met him, has she?"

Anne frowned at him, disturbed by his strange reaction. "No, I do not believe so. It is my understanding that her knowledge of the man comes completely from his mother. It is why I wished to speak to you about him."

Richard brought his laughter under control only with strict self-control. He knew it was necessary because of the increasing agitation on Anne's face. He got the impression she did not appreciate being on the receiving end of his humor.

To be fair, he would have felt similarly in her place. It was not pleasant to have Lady Catherine trying to control your life, especially when it was something as important as your marriage prospects. If Lady Catherine had set it up herself, she could not have picked a more ridiculous man to set her sights on.

Gyles Bellingham may have seemed like the perfect suitor from a strictly academic undertaking. He was wealthy, genuinely well-liked among the Ton, with vast holdings and a good head for business on his shoulders. Richard had even heard him described as handsome among the young ladies of the Ton. He was respectable, moderate in his habits.

By all outward appearances, he was a fine catch, and he might very well make a fine husband for some woman someday, but it would take the right person to temper his personality, and Lady Catherine was not it.

Richard swallowed his mirth. "Gyles is a fine enough young man, notable for one great fault. He is stubborn to his own detriment. When he has decided something is to be one way, he will cut off his nose before admitting he is wrong. He rarely takes advice, and has a penchant for stating his own opinions loudly and turning a deaf ear to all logic otherwise."

Anne's mouth rounded as she understood what that meant for her immediate future. "Oh." She grimaced, wrinkling her nose distastefully. "Oh, my. This is going to be rather difficult, is it not?"

Richard could not help chuckling. "Very. Like I said, he really is a pleasant fellow, as long as you do not disagree with him. However, Lady Catherine-"

He broke off with a helpless shrug and she finished his thought, "Is almost certain to disagree with him."

This time she was the one who chuckled and he was glad to see her able to find the humor in the situation. "Mother does not know what she has gotten herself into."

He shook his head, grinning. "No."

She folded her hands in her lap. "Well. If nothing else, I cannot complain that Kent is dull this spring."

"You certainly cannot say that," Fitzwilliam agreed. "This spring might even rival last year when we had Darcy and Elizabeth around to entertain us."

"It just might. I shall not know what to do with myself."

A commotion in the aisle caught both of their attentions. Since Richard was still holding the bridle, Anne rose to see what it was all about. Hansen stood in the doorway of the stable, talking to one of the head grooms. Aware the maid was probably looking for her, Anne nudged Andronicus out of the way and stepped into the aisle. "Do you need me, Hansen?"

The maid's head swung around, relief crossing her distressed face. "Yes, Miss de Bourgh. Your mother does not want the gown altered, but we have already started the process and we cannot repair what has already been done."

Anne heaved a sigh. Her pleasant interlude with Richard was over. "Very well. Let me talk to Mother about it and see what can be done." She glanced back at her cousin, who had resumed his work on the bridle. "I shall see you at dinner?"

His smile told her he would. "Try to remain calm in the intervening hours. I will be in as soon as I have finished this to entertain your mother."

What he really meant was that he would distract her. His offer was generous, and she did not argue, simply nodded her thanks and followed the maid out.

It took them nearly until dinner time to work out the alterations. During that time, Richard was an invaluable aid, lending his support to the changes they wished to make and convincing Lady Catherine that their design would have a much greater effect on the masculine psyche than any of her suggestions. And since her ultimate goal was Gyles' attraction to her daughter, she was more than happy to go along with what he told her would do the job.

His aid did much to smooth the waters between mother, daughter, and maids.

When Gyles arrived, Anne was in the midst of a frenzied fitting, with maids busy poking and prodding from all directions and her mother issuing orders left and right. Richard was the only one available to follow the butler down to the drawing room and receive him.

Mr. Gyles Bellingham grinned widely upon seeing him and offered him a firm handshake. "Good to see you, old man! Tell you what, I was not expecting to have you be the one to greet me after that summons from Lady Catherine. She all but demanded I show up, and when my mother tossed in her two cents I supposed I could handle a few days in Kent for their sakes."

Richard summoned a welcoming smile and took the hand he offered. "I was surprised to find you would be attending our little dinner party tonight. I do hope you will not find the country too tiresome after London."

Gyles grinned and pumped his hand. "If Miss de Bourgh is anything like Mother promised, it will be well worth the trip."

Richard stiffened at his remark, nerves prickling unexpectedly. He did not like the tone Gyles used, but he could not figure out why his protective instincts immediately went on high alert. He had known that the purpose of Gyles' presence was to further a match between him and Anne. Yet, it all seemed so utterly wrong. Anne was not meant to be with this man. But how could he say so? It was not his place. It was Anne and Lady Catherine's. All he could do was smile tightly and say, "My cousin is a remarkable woman."

Anne's inheritance of Rosings made her an attractive prospect for a bride, but she was so much more than her wealth. She was funny and wry, with a hidden passion that brought fire to her eyes and color to her cheeks. Would Gyles appreciate those parts of her? Richard was not sure.

He invited the man to take a seat so they could catch up while his bags were taken up to his room and until the women could join them.

Once he was settled by the fire, Gyles asked, "So what can you tell me about your cousin and her mother? My mother is convinced that Lady Catherine is always completely correct, but I am not so convinced. Still, I cannot help but admit that this is a lovely property. It would be quite a coup to unite our estates and families. My mother is all atwitter over the idea. She is convinced it is passed time I found a bride and I actually agree with her. Men of my age need a pretty young thing on their arm to make you older chaps take us seriously."

Richard clenched his fists around the arms of his chair to keep himself from throttling the young man. Of all the pompous, arrogant… "My cousin is not a possession, you know. She has a mind of her own and a remarkable head for figures."

Gyles brushed that off. "That is all very fine and good. I am sure she will do wonders running a household, but she need not worry about figures when I take over Rosings. What I should like to inspect is *her* figure." He said it with raised eyebrows and a laugh that told Richard he fully expected him to understand the sentiment.

Instead, Richard's blood ran cold. Gyles did not realize just how close he was to being strangled in that moment. He started, "I-"

Thankfully, Lady Catherine chose that moment to make her grand entrance, breezing in the door in a cloud of taffeta and perfume with a wide smile and eyes only for Gyles. She exclaimed, "My dear, dear, boy!" and smothered the young man in an entirely unexpected hug.

Even Darcy had never been greeted with such enthusiasm. It was quite out of character for his usually fastidious aunt, and it took them all by surprise.

When Gyles eventually emerged from her bosom, he looked shell-shocked and more than a little oxygen deprived. Richard could not help but smile with no small satisfaction. The man deserved whatever man-handling he got at Lady Catherine's hands. Richard crossed his arms over his chest. Until Gyles had arrived, he had felt some sympathy for the man, facing off against his aunt as he was, but now his sympathy belonged solely to Anne.

This was the man he had defended as a good man only a few hours earlier to Anne. How could he have been so mistaken?

If Gyles could not appreciate her for more than her property or her figure, he did not deserve her. Richard had no reason to further any match between them and he had no desire to.

Since Lady Catherine had arrived and had the situation firmly in hand, Richard excused himself and headed up to his rooms, thinking he needed a few minutes to himself to regain his composure before he had to come back down for dinner.

Anne was just exiting her room as he passed, clad in the peach gown. The sight of her stopped him in his tracks and stole all the air from his lungs. He could not tear his eyes away from her.

She fidgeted with her skirts nervously. "What is it? Do I have something on me?"

He swallowed hard. "You look beautiful. Absolutely divine."

The peach color of the gown brought out the color in her cheeks and offset the magnificent fall of her hair over one shoulder. And her eyes…they sparkled with life and animation. He had never seen another woman that could hold a candle to her in that moment. Not even Elizabeth Darcy with all her wit and charm had ever captured his attention like she did.

The pink in her cheeks deepened. "Thank you. I hope Mother approves. We had to shorten the sleeves like she did not want us to do."

It was hard to focus on her words, but Richard managed to close his gaping mouth long enough to concentrate on her voice. "I am sure she will not even notice, now that Gyles is here. She is already quite distracted by her eagerness to welcome him."

Anne smoothed a hand over her stomach, brows puckering into a frown. "Gyles is here? And alone with Mother?" She cast a worried glance at the staircase he had just come up. "That cannot be good."

Richard was irrationally irritated by her concern for Gyles. He said, "On the contrary, it is probably in their best interests. Let them get a lay of the land, so to speak, without any interference from us. If anything is to come from this visit, surely they would have to learn how to interact properly without coming to blows over every little thing."

She giggled, apparently amused by the thought of her mother and potential suitor coming to blows. Little did she know, thought Richard ruefully. It just might come to that if they were not careful.

Of course, those blows might be exchanged between Richard and Gyles and not Lady Catherine and Gyles if their brief conversation was any harbinger…

He sighed. "Gyles will be so overwhelmed by the sight of you in that dress that he will forget anything your mother might say."

"Do you really think so?" Anne glanced down at herself, doubt crossing her face.

Was she really so concerned about impressing Gyles? The man did not deserve her concern. His irritation flared again and then settled as he realized the origin of her concerns. Anne was so used to blending in to a room that she was worried about standing out. She had spent most of her life trying to hide from attention. It was against her nature to seek it.

His heart softened. It was not wrong for his cousin to attract attention. Indeed, she had certainly snagged his, and entirely without intending to. It was not her fault that Gyles was such a fool. She had not yet even met the man. All she knew was what Richard had told her, and he only had himself to blame for the inaccuracies in that portrayal.

Every young girl dreamed of getting married, did she not? Of course Anne would desire that for herself. For all she knew, Gyles could be the man who made that dream a reality. Richard fervently hoped she realized it was not going to happen before it was too late. She would not be happy with a man who did not appreciate her for who she was.

Still, it really was not any of his business who she married. However, he reassured himself that as her cousin, it was well within his role to be concerned for her happiness. He would make sure that Gyles treated her with the respect she deserved while he was at Rosings, even if he could not control what might happen after he left.

"I know so," he told her honestly. Still, he was not ready for Gyles to see her looking so fetching. "I had a question I wanted to ask you about one of the tenants. Do you have a few minutes to go over it with me?"

She cast another look at the stairs. "Do you think I should? Will not Mother be expecting me to welcome our guest?"

Richard took her by the elbow and nudged her in the opposite direction, toward the study he had taken over upon his arrival. "Do not worry yourself about Gyles. I believe your mother wished to speak to him privately while his bags were being brought up, then she was going to give him a chance to change and wash up before dinner. I am sure they will both want for him to be at his best when he meets you."

"You are most likely correct," she agreed, letting him lead her up the hall. "That does sound like Mother's reasoning. She certainly wanted me to be at my best."

"And you are," Richard complimented her. "Your mother will be proud to show off your beauty. However, right now I need your brains to be on full display."

He opened the door to his study and escorted her in, seating her in the chair behind the desk. He pulled up a chair of his own close to hers, until their elbows brushed as she turned the pages of the ledger and the scent of her perfume filled his nostrils.

He reached over her arm to point out the tenant he was curious about, a current of electricity making the hairs of his arm stand on end as his fingers grazed hers. "This is the one I wanted to know about."

The brush of his skin against Anne's sent her heart into arrhythmia. Her nerves jangled and then settled as he withdrew his hand. She reminded herself to breathe and tried to concentrate on the question he had just asked. What strange illness was befalling her body now? She had never felt like this, dizzy and lightheaded as her nostrils caught a whiff of his cologne. If this continued, she might have to beg off from dinner. Fortunately, her symptoms eased as Richard shifted away from her, sitting back in his seat so he could listen intently to what she had to say.

Richard smiled and nodded as she explained, feeling the tension in his muscles slowly ease. She really was very good at this.

It was an entirely unnecessary undertaking, as Richard had already had the steward explain the whole situation to him. However, it allowed him to relax and listen to her soothing voice, knowing she was safe from Gyles' clutches for the time being.

However, even his delaying tactics could not keep her from meeting the man eventually. As he knew was inevitable, the butler knocked on the study door and cleared his throat to capture their attention.

Anne looked up with a smile. "Yes?"

"Lady Catherine requires your presence in the parlor," he intoned seriously. "Mr. Bellingham and Mr. and Mrs. Collins have arrived. Dinner will be served in a quarter of an hour."

"Very well," Anne replied graciously. "We shall be down momentarily."

The butler nodded and disappeared, leaving Richard and Anne to eye each other, both disappointed that their brief respite together had come to an end but unwilling to admit it aloud.

Finally, Richard cleared his throat. "I appreciate you taking the time to explain this matter to me. It has been most helpful."

Anne nodded, and cast her eyes back down to the ledger. "Certainly. I should be happy to be of assistance at any time." She carefully eased the ledger closed, the whisper of the pages the only noise in the room. She rose gracefully with one hand still on the leather binding. "Are you ready to do this?"

Richard chuckled and reached over to take her dainty chin in his fingers. "The real question is, are *you* ready to do this?"

Anne's breath caught and awareness flickered between them. Richard dropped his hand and stepped away hurriedly. He would not put a name to what had just passed between them but he recognized the spark of attraction that flared to life whenever she was near.

He could only hope she did not. Her mother had decided she was destined to become Mrs. Anne Bellingham, and until Anne decided otherwise, he could not interfere. He would not interfere. It would not be fair to her or to Gyles.

He would always support Anne. He had a feeling it was going to be a lifelong habit regardless of what the future held for either one of them.

Anne tucked a loose strand of hair behind her ear and glanced up at him from under her eyelashes, stealing another little piece of his heart with her shy gaze. That look was such a juxtaposition from her usually straight forward, open gaze. What was she thinking? He could not bear to know.

Groaning inside, he forced a smile to his lips. "Come. Let us go down before they start to wonder where we have gone off to."

He lifted a hand to signal she should precede him, then followed her into the hall. He did not dare to offer her his arm or take her elbow to assist her down the stairs. He knew she did not really need any assistance. It was his own traitorous heart that wanted to offer it to her.

If she wondered at his lack of chivalry, she did not comment. Instead, she was silent, troubled, as they traversed the empty hallways to the parlor.

It did not take them long to reach the heavy oak doors that separated them from the rest of the mixed company. Anne put her hand out to open them, but Richard stopped her with a hand on her shoulder. He could not let her go in there without some reassurance.

He looked down at her with serious eyes. "You look beautiful. Do not let anyone tell you otherwise. And do not let Gyles make you uncomfortable. He can come across very strong and overbearing, much like your mother. You have experience handling that, but it is different when you are contemplating someone as a husband and not as a parent."

Unexpectedly touched by his words, she patted his shoulder. "Thank you, Richard. You are a good friend to me."

With that, she opened the door and walked in the drawing room, leaving him to follow with a false smile pasted on his face.

You are a good friend to me. A friend. Yes. Right. That was all they were ever meant to be. Friends. And cousins. Why did that suddenly feel so wrong? Like it was not quite enough?

Dissatisfied, and with no more answers than he had started out with, he greeted the other people gathered in the room. Mr. Collins was perched near Lady Catherine, looking thrilled to be allowed in her presence. He was extolling her many virtues and his extreme gratitude to her to Mr. Bellingham, while his wife sat silent and uncomfortable nearby.

Richard did not think that her discomfort was entirely due to her husband's ridiculousness. The woman was heavily pregnant. Richard surmised that she might be due to give birth at any moment from the way she shifted uncomfortably in her chair and surreptitiously rubbed at her lower back. If it had been his wife, he would have immediately sent her home and packed her into bed until the woman presented him with a child.

Gyles was watching the whole tableau play out in front of him with a sardonic gleam in his eye and private humor, but when Anne appeared in the doorway, he immediately rose to his feet and bowed over her hand appreciatively as the introductions were made. His smile was smooth and charming. "Miss de Bourgh, you are a vision this evening."

Anne flushed to the roots of her hair at his compliment. She murmured in response, "Thank you, Mr. Bellingham. It is a pleasure to make your acquaintance. My mother has been most eager to introduce you."

"As I have been most eager to be introduced, I assure you," said Gyles.

Richard covered his snort with a cough and went to take a seat beside the poor Mrs. Collins. Someone needed to keep an eye on the lady. It might as well be him, since no one else seemed inclined to take the job, least of all her husband. He was too busy attending to another lady at the moment.

Lady Catherine frowned at him. "Richard," she said sharply, "I do hope you have not caught a cold. That is the second time I have heard you cough."

"It is nothing catching, I promise," he said, with a wry tilt to his lips. He shared a glance with Anne, who hid a smile of her own behind a hand.

"I should hope not," said Lady Catherine. She switched her attention to Mr. Bellingham. "You know I would never allow anyone to endanger my Anne. Her health is of the utmost importance to me, Mr. Bellingham."

"Miss de Bourgh appears to be in excellent health," said Gyles approvingly, his gaze still on the lovely woman in question. He could not seem to tear his eyes away from her.

Richard could not fault him there, as much as he would have liked to be able to, he thought grumpily. He had had the same reaction when he had first seen her. She was stunning.

Mr. Collins broke in, "My dear Lady Catherine. Your concern for your daughter does you a great justice. Such familial loyalty and care is too often neglected in our society. How refreshing to see one of your magnitude and authority showing such care! I would expect nothing less from your ladyship, of course, for your concern is bestowed most generously, beyond the bounds of society's expectations. If only all would be as loving as your ladyship is, my work would be much simpler. As it is, I will only have to point to your ladyship as the perfect example to be imitated by all the parish and much will be improved. I think I must speak on the topic this Sunday and uphold the many virtues of the family bond."

"You would do much better to lecture them on the merits of avoiding a cold," said Lady Catherine, in a tone that brooked no disagreement. "Illness is unholy. Those who are ill should be cast outside the camp, like they did to those in the Old Testament."

Gyles was the first to recover from this shocking statement, opening his mouth to respond with what was sure to be an equally controversial statement.

Thankfully, the butler appeared in the doorway just then and intoned drolly, "Dinner is served, my lady."

Lady Catherine rose immediately. "Very good. Richard, you will see me in. Mr. Bellingham, you may lead in my daughter. And Mr. Collins, you must see to your wife."

Mr. Collins appeared quite disappointed to have the honor of leading in Lady Catherine relegated to her nephew, but he bore the dishonor well, scurrying over to heave his wife out of the deep seat she had settled in to.

His pull propelled her forward into him, her round belly catching him in the torso and knocking the air out of his lungs. Richard was almost impressed that Mr. Collins had the strength required to pull her up like that. Unfortunately, he did not recover from the strain well. His eyes bulged as he doubled over and gasped for air. His wife reached consoling hands to him but he pushed her away. "You have done quite enough, woman!" he wheezed.

"Mr. Collins!" Lady Catherine reprimanded him. "That is quite enough! I told you to see your wife into dinner, and so you shall do!"

Mrs. Collins dropped her hands as pain sliced through her abdomen. She grabbed for her stomach at the same time her husband straightened and reached for her arm. "Oh!"

For a pregnant woman, there was only one thing that sound and stance could mean.

The entire room erupted into a chaos that Lady Catherine quickly tried to shout down.

"Are you alright?!" Anne rushed forward.

"Someone call the doctor," Richard instructed, calmly helping Mrs. Collins back into her chair.

"Oh, dear. Oh, dear," said Mr. Collins to no one in particular. He wrung his hands and glanced from one face to another, quite unsure what to do with himself.

"Be quiet! I said, be quiet!" When her raised voice failed to illicit any response from the people gathered around Mrs. Collins, Lady Catherine pounded her cane against the floor. She boomed, "Hush! When I ask for silence, I expect silence!"

She got it, for one long second before Gyles broke out laughing in a loud booming laugh that was incongruous with the seriousness of the situation. "This has got to be one of the most ridiculous scenes I have ever beheld."

Everyone in the room turned to glare at him, but Lady Catherine's gaze was the most heated of all.

She banged her cane against the floor once more. "Young man, I expect respect in this household." Her glare finally silenced him, although a grin remained. She chose to ignore it. "Now, let us all go in to dinner before the meal grows cold. Mr. Bellingham, you may escort in my daughter."

Richard and Anne shared a stricken glance. Beside them, Mrs. Collins panted through a contraction.

"Mother," stated Anne carefully, "perhaps it would be best if we called for the carriage to be brought round for Mr. and Mrs. Collins. Or at the very least, we should call for the doctor."

"Nonsense," said Lady Catherine, turning her back to go in to dinner. "If Mr. and Mrs. Collins were to go home it would throw off our numbers. They cannot leave now. Richard, you must escort me in or I shall have Mr. Collins do the job for you."

Mr. Collins immediately brightened and scuttled forward eagerly, his wife completely forgotten. "I would be honored to escort you in to dine Lady Catherine."

When after a few seconds pause Richard showed no inclination to come to her assistance, Lady Catherine took his arm and the pair disappeared in the direction of the dining room.

Gyles followed them to the doorway and then stood there with raised eyebrows, waiting expectantly for Anne to join him. Anne gaped at his audaciousness and then looked back at the remaining pair.

"Oh, for goodness' sakes!" growled Richard under his breath. He reached for Mrs. Collins' hands. "Can you sit through dinner or shall I call for the doctor and have you set up in a room?"

She groaned as the contraction eased off. "My husband will never forgive me if I ruin one of Lady Catherine's dinner parties."

"It is not your husband you should be concerned about right now," Richard said firmly. "It is your child."

Mrs. Collins bit her lip, looking uncertain. "Lady Catherine has advised me many times that a woman's first child often takes many hours to make its appearance into the world. I am sure that a little discomfort will not hurt me or my child and my presence will ultimately make things easier for all involved."

Richard was not sure how much easier it would really be and he was horrified that everyone seemed to be just fine going in to a dinner party while one of the guests was in labor. Of all his aunt's outlandish feats, this had to be one of the most ridiculous. It was even more ridiculous that everyone was going along with it.

The only good thing that could come of this was the possibility that they might have a healthy baby by the time the dessert course was served.

"Well," he said, "I cannot stop you from proceeding as you wish. However, I would like to speak with the butler and make sure a room is ready and the doctor is on standby should you need him. Would that be agreeable to you?"

Anne seemed relieved by the suggestion, although Mrs. Collins wavered before accepting it. "I suppose that would be an acceptable course of action, although my husband will not like to inconvenience Lady Catherine."

"It will be no inconvenience at all," reassured Anne. "Lately my mother has been waxing poetic on the pleasure of a new baby at Rosings. She will not be upset to have one a little earlier than she had planned." If she was, Anne would make sure that Mrs. Collins never learned of it. There was more than one way to convince her mother it was in her best interests to host the woman should she be unable to make it home.

And since she had insisted on staying for dinner, it was pretty much guaranteed that this baby would be born at Rosings, not the parsonage.

Although he did not like it, Richard carefully helped Mrs. Collins to her feet, then offered her an arm to lean on. She propped herself heavily on him as they crossed the parlor with Anne following closely behind. He felt the strain in her with every step, but he managed to keep his mouth closed and his opinion locked inside by setting his lips into a grim line. He wanted to shake some sense into his aunt. Barring that, he wanted to shake some sense into Mr. Collins and his poor wife. Since he did not have those options, he settled for offering up a quick prayer for the safe and healthy arrival of the child Mrs. Collins carried.

Gyles was still waiting impatiently for Anne in the doorway as they passed. He gave her a charming grin and held out his arm to her. "May I, Miss de Bourgh?"

Since her only other option would have been to deliberately ignore him and go in to dinner on her own, which would have been considered unaccountably rude, she took the arm he offered her. "Just allow me a moment to speak with the butler in the hall. I must make sure we have a room prepared and call for the doctor."

"I am sure that is not really necessary," said Gyles. "As Mrs. Collins said, firstborn children often take their time arriving."

Stifling her irritation with his illogic, she gave him a tight smile. Could men really be expected to know the ways of women and babies? "I prefer to be prepared for all contingencies."

As they made their way down the hall, the butler came hurrying toward them, having been sent back by Richard.

Anne stopped in her tracks, forcing Gyles to stop with her as a gentleman should. She turned a beguiling smile on the servant. "Ah! Good! I did so wish to speak with you. I know you will be able to be of the utmost assistance. Mrs. Collins' time has come, but she wishes to remain at dinner for the time being. Could you please make sure that a room is set aside for her use and the doctor is called for? I wish to have him in the building should she have need of him at any time."

The butler bowed, apparently having perceived much of the situation himself, and offered her his most grave assurances that all would be done just as she had requested.

"You have a very dedicated staff," Gyles commented as they moved on, allowing the butler to hurry off to his duties.

"Yes," she acknowledged. "We are most fortunate. Not many could say the same about their staff. I do my best to make sure they know their hard work is appreciated. When the servants know they are appreciated, it makes it much more unlikely they will go looking for positions elsewhere. We prefer to promote from within, which encourages loyalty as well, and ensures that there is minimal fuss when changes are made since our servants are already familiar with how the household is run."

"It still must be difficult to keep them from gossiping," Gyles commented with a grin. "Everyone knows how servants love to gossip among themselves. Why, my visit will probably be the talk of the town before the night is over." He almost seemed pleased with the idea.

Anne frowned at his supposition. "On the contrary, I assure you, our staff understands the need for discretion. While your visit may be spoken about in the village, it will be because many saw you ride through town, not because of the loose lips of our staff."

His smile disappeared, as though he could sense her disapproval of him. "You defend them most admirably."

She glanced at him from the corner of her eye, trying to judge what he might be thinking. She did not know him well enough to trust him yet. "They have earned my admiration. As you said, they are most dedicated."

"Indeed," he agreed, but she got the impression that he was not quite as agreeable about her defense of them.

The conversation went no further as they entered the dining room and Gyles led her to her seat, pulling out the chair for her and making sure she was settled comfortably before he found his own chair. In all that passed, she could not fault his manners. His actions were those of a well-bred gentleman. But his speech… she was not so sure she could approve of all he had said. Perhaps it was not so much the words he used, which were not ill-mannered in and of themselves, but his tone and insinuation. He seemed to be saying more than what the words that came from his mouth expressed. She felt he was hiding something from her, although she could not for the life of her figure out what that might be. He had no valid reason to hide anything from her. In her mother's eyes they were as good as married. Yet, Anne was not so sure. Especially when she glanced down the table and her gaze caught on Richard's.

The worry in his eyes made her breath hitch. Not because he was concerned about Mrs. Collins. Oh no. That worry in his eyes had nothing to do with the pregnant woman and everything to do with the interaction between her and Gyles. And it made her smile just to realize it.

His gaze warmed at her smile. The awareness that flickered between them again was an alive thing, jumping and sparking across the table in such a way that it was a wonder the meal managed to go on around them. The tension connecting them was only broken when Mrs.

Collins gasped and clutched a fistful of the tablecloth as she began to pant through a contraction. Richard turned to give her his full and undivided attention.

The man really did have an incredible way about him. Anne was impressed by his attentiveness to Mrs. Collins, even when it seemed that everyone else around the table was determined to ignore her intermittent gasps of pain as each contraction hit.

Gyles drew Anne's attention back to him by plying her with a question, "Do tell me, Miss de Bourgh, which of these fine dishes laid out before us is your favorite?"

Anne surveyed the meal spread out before them, noticing for the first time that all her favorite dishes were on the table. Her mother must have been trying to curry her good behavior with food. Unfortunately, that probably meant the kitchen had been overworked and the household budget stretched. It was a good thing she had built in some room in the budget for unexpected expenditures. With her mother in residence, there always seemed to be expenses popping up she did not count on.

"It seems my mother has been busy," Anne said. "I could not choose a favorite from among these, for the dishes can all be counted among my favorites."

"Surely there is one that stands out above the others," said he.

Anne forced a smile to her lips. "As I told you earlier, our staff is quite competent. Our cook is no exception. I could not risk offending her by choosing one dish above another."

And so the meal went. Gyles plied her with question upon meaningless question, while Mr. Collins plied Lady Catherine with compliments and Richard tried to keep Mrs. Collins calm as her labor progressed. Somehow, Mrs.

Collins managed to keep her composure, up until the time the gentlemen rose to go to their port.

Just as the men stood, she let out a very undignified squawk and leaned forward to grab the edge of the table in a death grip. She gasped, "I think you had best call for the doctor now."

The men froze in their tracks, half out of their chairs, and looked at each other, uncertain what to do. Even Lady Catherine paused with her wine glass halfway to her lips.

Men. They were useless when you needed them. With an indignant huff, Anne pushed back her chair and hurried around the table. She put an encouraging arm around Mrs. Collins' shoulders and crooned, "I sent for the doctor before we came into dinner. Let us just get you upstairs to the room we have prepared for you so he can attend you."

Shakily, Mrs. Collins managed to heft herself out of the chair. The men watched warily as she took Anne's arm. She took two steps toward the door before grabbing her stomach. She groaned as fluid puddled on the floor beneath her.

Mr. Collins went pale.

Gyles gaped at the puddle. "Did that come from her?"

Mr. Collins managed to squeak out, "Is-" Then he hit the floor.

Gyles swallowed hard and sank back down in his chair, looking a little green around the gills. "I have never..." His eyes rolled back in his head and he slumped over in his chair.

Now they had two men down for the count. Anne rolled her eyes and glanced at Richard. Was he soon to follow? He still looked like he had all his color. He returned her steady gaze. He was strong, sturdy, even in this situation. His mouth quirked up. "It seems we now have two more patients for our doctor. He will be a busy man tonight."

She chuckled, caught off guard by his humor. "He will certainly earn his wages. Can you help me get Mrs. Collins upstairs, or will you be the next patient for our physician?"

Richard laughed. "You need not worry. I have seen much worse."

Lady Catherine set down her fork and said sharply, "Where are you going? I will not have my dinner party disrupted in such a way! Do you know the time and expense that has gone into this meal?! You must stay until the gentlemen can have their port, at the very least. Surely, Mrs. Collins can last a little while longer. She has been fine this long." She raised her voice in a huff. "Someone get in here to clean up this mess!"

The remaining members of the party ignored her, even as the butler hurried in. Quickly sizing up the situation, he promptly disappeared again, presumably to fetch the doctor from wherever he had stashed the man.

Richard moved to join Anne, being careful to avoid the puddle on the floor as he took Mrs. Collins' elbow. Together, one on each side, they managed to help her to the stairs and slowly climb them, pausing frequently to allow her to pant through a contraction.

Considering how slowly they moved, the doctor was able to meet them halfway up the stairs, converse with Mrs. Collins briefly, and disappear again to see to the men. By the time they had reached the upper landing, he had returned.

"The men are resting comfortably in the parlor for the time being. I will return to check on them after I have seen you settled." The man kept up a running commentary as they continued down the hall. "You will appreciate the room Miss de Bourgh has chosen for us. It is warm and cozy and the fire has been built up to keep it nice and toasty in there. She has had all the linens and the bed prepared for you. You are fortunate to have such a wonderful hostess to care for you. It will be much more comfortable here at Rosings than it would be at the parsonage. Before you know it, your new son or daughter will be here. Will that not be wonderful?"

Mrs. Collins managed a groan in response that the doctor took to be agreement.

"Once your new son or daughter is born, all this difficulty will be all but forgotten. I have seen it time and time again with new mothers. They welcome one child and they are ready to bear the next."

"Please, no!" Mrs. Collins interjected. "I cannot bear the thought of that right now."

The doctor chuckled. "Of course. You would say that at the moment. Just wait. You will be singing a different tune soon enough. When you have that babe in your arms you will not begrudge your husband more children."

Mrs. Collins shot him a look of pure hatred, but somehow managed to hold her tongue. Richard and Anne shared a look, but neither of them spoke. They knew better than to weigh in on either opinion.

Thankfully, they had reached Mrs. Collin's room at that moment. The doctor opened the door for them, then followed them inside. He helped them settle Mrs. Collins into the bed, which they managed to accomplish without much conversation. One of the upstairs maids had been assigned to care for any of the needs the doctor or Mrs. Collins might have, and she hurried forward as Anne stepped away, ready and eager to help.

The doctor quickly took over. Anne and Richard backed out of the room, glad to let the professional take charge. When the door finally closed behind them, they paused to catch their breath before they had to face the men and Lady Catherine still downstairs.

Richard turned to Anne with a wry smile. "I told you dinner would not be dull."

She laughed, one short burst issuing from her. "You did promise me excitement. However, I do not think this was what you had in mind."

Richard chuckled. "No. Not even I could have foreseen this. Mrs. Collins' timing is impeccable. Only she could ruin your mother's dinner party by choosing to have her child tonight. At least in the end, there will be a baby to coax your mother out of her temper tantrum."

"That is a fitting end," agreed Anne. She sighed and rubbed at her forehead. "What are we going to do with Mr. Collins and Gyles? As much as I would like to, we cannot just send them home."

"No, I very much fear we are stuck with them. It would not be good form to send the father home while his wife has a baby upstairs, even if he is less than helpful."

Anne snorted. "Less than helpful? He fainted in the middle of the dining room. I assume it might be a common occurrence for first time fathers, but it is certainly a first for Rosings. I am sure the story will be repeated for years to come."

"I am sure Gyles will be embarrassed that he followed suit soon after," said Richard. And he was not too sorry about that himself.

Anne shook her head. "I am sure. The men were more trouble than the woman having the baby. Please tell me I can expect greater things from your sex in the future."

Richard grinned. "I make no such promises. I never make a promise I cannot keep, and I am nearly certain that at one time or another in the not too distant future, Mr. Collins or Mr. Bellingham will disappoint you. I can only hope that I will not be counted among their number."

She smiled and teased, "You are holding up admirably so far, although you failed to jump into action when I expected you to."

"I was only trying to be certain it was not a false alarm before I reacted," he asserted with a smile that told her he was not taking himself too seriously. She appreciated that about him. He was never the one who had to be right. He was willing to admit his mistakes and work to correct them, and he was willing to laugh at himself. It had been a long time since she had known anyone who would do all those things. Her mother certainly never did, and if early indications proved to be true, Gyles did not.

Anne propped herself against the wall, leaning her head back to let it rest on the crimson paper that lined the hall. The colors here were warm, even if the atmosphere was not always. She smiled up at Richard, who lounged a few feet away on the opposite side of the hall. He let the wall hold him up, crossing his long legs and booted feet in front of him. She said, "I thought we had established before we went in to dinner that this was not a false alarm."

He chuckled. "Touché, madam." He uncrossed his legs and straightened. "I suppose we must go down. Mr. Collins will be expecting news, not that we have much to give him. I fear the next few hours will involve keeping the soon-to-be father calm more than anything else."

"It would have been much simpler if he had just stayed home with his wife," Anne said with a sigh. She was not as eager to give up the comfort of her position slouched against the wall for the discomfort of the parlor. "I do not understand the power my mother has over him."

"Truly?" Richard said with a chuckle. "I understand that fear. Although, I must say, my presence here has more to do with family expectations than any true fear of your mother. I almost envy Darcy his disassociation at times."

He turned a warm smile on her. "Yet, if I had suffered that fate as well, I would not have this time with you, my dear cousin. I must say, the effort is worth the reward at the moment."

She warmed under his gaze, feeling the blush creep into her cheeks. Eyes downcast, she pushed away from the wall. "I am glad you chose to come. It would be dreadfully difficult right now without you."

She turned to go down the hall, but he stopped her with a hand on her elbow. "I have not done much," he told her, his gaze suddenly intense. "But what I have done has all been for you."

Her breath came short and fast and she suddenly yearned for a future she could not have. Her mother had brought Gyles here to Rosings in the hopes of securing a future for her with him. It was Gyles she should be yearning for, Gyles she should be standing in the hall with.

Yet it was not Gyles who spoke to her heart. Hating herself for her defection and the confusion she knew she was wreaking in Richard's heart, she stretched up on to her tippy toes and pressed a very sisterly kiss to her cousin's cheek. "You are a good man, Richard Fitzwilliam. Better than I deserve. You have been a good friend to me." Then she patted him on the shoulder and walked off down the hall to find Gyles and Mr. Collins.

Richard watched her go, one hand raised to the spot on his cheek she had kissed.

CHAPTER FIVE

Richard Fitzwilliam was jealous.

It was unfortunate that he knew what name to give the riotous feelings swelling and ebbing in his chest, for he would have dearly liked to ignore them and go on pretending they did not exist.

He fought the urge to glare at the gentleman currently holding court over Anne's attention. The gentleman in question, Gyles, certainly seemed to be enjoying himself. He had been going on and on for ages in response to a simple question she had posed. Really, who could talk for fifteen minutes about the merits of shoes over boots? He glanced at his feet. He only owned one pair of shoes, for dress occasions, and they were rarely used. Boots were far more practical.

He reached for his cup of tea again, wishing for something stronger. Coffee might have made this conversation bearable.

It had been a long night, and he was not sure the end of it was in sight yet.

Mr. Collins had gone up to see his wife and new daughter an hour ago. Lady Catherine had retired in a fit of pique once she had realized her dinner party had disintegrated around her and that nobody was paying her any mind, not even her beloved Mr. Collins. It did not seem to matter to her that the man had been passed out cold at the time.

Both he and Mr. Bellingham had made a quick recovery once the good doctor had moved them out of the dining room and brought out his smelling salts. Unfortunately, neither Mr. Collins nor Mr. Bellingham had had the good sense to be embarrassed by their lack of fortitude. They seemed to think their reaction was natural for men dealing with female ailments. Richard, however, thought it was never very masculine to faint dead away and then leave the mess for the women to clean up.

It was not easy to keep his mouth shut, but he managed to do so, mostly by drinking cup after cup of tea. He set down his empty cup again and reached for the pot. Before he could pour for himself, Anne, ever the hostess, took the cup from him and filled it once more. When she set down the teapot, it was almost empty. Again. She rose fluidly to ring for another pot, managing to do it all without leaving Gyles in the lurch. Again, an unfortunate thing, that.

Richard would have loved to have seen how he would react if she was to divide up her attention. He had a feeling the man was not used to being ignored. Gyles probably would not take it well.

He sighed as he swallowed another sip of tea, giving Anne a nod of thanks. She had made sure his tea was just the way he liked it, despite his bad humor.

He was not usually a petty man. It was just this jealousy was eating him alive. He did not know what to do about it. It was such a foreign emotion for him. He had never felt this way before about a woman. About anyone or anything, really.

Sure, he had gone through a bit of jealousy growing up when he had realized the differences that stood between him and his older brother. In a family, there was a great disparity between what was expected of a first son and a second son. His brother's future was laid out before him with ease. He would never have to worry or scrape by. Mothers would be pleased to have his attention focused on their daughters.

However, things would not be so simple for him as a second son. He would be expected to find a vocation and make a living, support himself on his own funds and not out of the family coffers. Mothers would spurn his advances. There was little he could have offered a woman until he had sold his commission. Even now he knew there were many who would refuse to give him their daughter's hand in marriage. If he chose to marry, it would have to be for the depth of a woman's pockets or the size of her dowry, not necessarily for love. Richard was not sure he could make that choice, which was why he was still unmarried and at his Aunt Catherine's beck and call.

Still, that did not mean he wanted to remain that way for the rest of his life.

He felt his hand tighten uncomfortably around the delicate china cup and readjusted his grip. He looked down into the murky depths of his tea and felt like he was looking into the depths of his soul. When had he become so confused and mixed up? He knew when. It was when Anne had walked into his life again. Or perhaps more correctly, when he had rode Andronicus through the gates of Rosings earlier in the week.

He could not afford to lose his heart to her when she was losing her heart to someone else. He did not know what she wanted for her future, what hopes and dreams she held dear. Other than her passion for roses, he really knew very little about her, the real her at least. He knew quite a bit about the woman he had assumed she was. But now he knew just how incorrect those assumptions had been. He would not make the same mistake again.

And he would not interfere in a budding romance, no matter how much his jealous heart might desire it.

The housekeeper appeared in the doorway in response to Anne's call, and this time she had a pot of coffee instead of tea. Richard perked up.

His cousin smiled at him. "I thought you might prefer something a little stronger."

The words so perfectly echoed his earlier thoughts that he was half afraid he had spoken them aloud. The serenity with which she smiled at him reassured him. There would have been a teasing gleam in her eye if he had mentioned the coffee. Draining his tea, he eagerly accepted a cup from her, although Gyles chose to keep his tea.

"The acidity of coffee does horrors to my stomach," he told them with a lazy smile. "I cannot stand the stuff."

Since Richard had often shared a cup with Anne over breakfast, he glanced at her, expecting some sort of response.

She just smiled genially. "Is it not pleasant how we all have our preferences? The world would be a very boring place if we all liked the same things."

Richard was reminded of how often she had spoken of bringing excitement to her dull life. Maybe what she wanted was a husband who spurned her every opinion, like Gyles was sure to do. She would certainly never be bored if that was the case, although Richard could not imagine what type of home life that would be. He certainly would not want it.

Gyles spoke up. "Oh, it is not simply a preference. I believe we would all be better off if we avoided acidic foods like coffee and oranges. I make sure my estate no longer stocks such supplies. You should really try it. I am sure it would help to heal whatever health ailments you have. Your mother has often spoke of your poor health."

Annoyance crossed Anne's face, flitting on and off before anyone besides Richard had the time to notice it. Even he would not have seen it if he had not happened to be looking directly at her when Gyles made the statement.

Anne filled her own cup from the coffee pot and sipped it deliberately. "Rumors of my poor health are greatly exaggerated. My mother worries unnecessarily. As Mr. Collins so graciously pointed out earlier, she is a great fan of advising her family members. Her familial loyalty is undisputed, as I am sure my cousin can testify. Is that not correct, Richard?"

Richard nearly choked on his coffee. He had not expected her to put him on the spot. He coughed and sat down his cup. "Your mother is concerned for her family above all things. They, in turn, put great store in her advice. Mr. Collins finds it invaluable while preparing his sermons. She is always very up-to-date on current happenings in the area."

Which was a very nice way of saying she was a busybody who always had her nose in other people's affairs. Gyles knew that as much as he did. What he did not realize was just how much he was alike Lady Catherine in that regard. Richard could see it. He wondered if Anne could, too. It would not surprise him if she did. However, what she would do with that information remained to be seen.

Gyles frowned at Anne as she sipped her coffee. He reached to take the cup from her. "Perhaps if you tried giving up the bad habit for a few days you would understand the wisdom of my suggestion."

"You give your opinions very decidedly," she told him, evading his grasping hands by holding the cup out of his reach.

"Only because I know them to be correct," he said firmly. Since he could not take her cup, he moved the coffee pot out of her reach, setting it on the other side of the tea tray. Richard resisted the urge to snort. As if that would stop them from drinking it, should they so desire.

Anne tried another tactic. "My mother has often stated her preference for a cup of coffee when the weather has turned chilly. She is convinced it wards off illness. She has prescribed it as just the remedy I need too many times for me to count."

"Any hot beverage would work just as well for that purpose," Gyles asserted.

Richard smiled around his cup. "Perhaps. However, would just any beverage be as satisfying? I think not."

Richard could tell his comment rankled Gyles, especially when Anne laughed and agreed. "There is something special about a cup of coffee that no other beverage can quite deliver. Even tea is not precisely the same."

Gyles looked ready to open his mouth and dispute that fact.

Anne cut him off with conciliatory smile. "Come now, Mr. Bellingham. Let us not argue. We must agree to disagree on this matter. I will ensure you always have your tea while you are here at Rosings, and Richard and I shall enjoy our coffee."

He did not look ready to acquiesce. Instead, he appeared to be considering the merits of debating the subject further.

Fortunately, Mr. Collins chose that moment to appear, distracting them from the topic for one of admittedly more importance and interest- the safe delivery of his wife and brand new daughter.

He scurried into the room on fast feet, bowing low in front of Anne. "Miss de Bourgh, you must accept my apologies for being absent for so long. Is your dear mother able to come down for a time? I would dearly like to discuss a matter of the greatest importance with her."

"What would you like to ask her?" said Anne. "I am sure that she will not mind being disturbed if the matter is of great importance, but I would not like to wake her this early if it truly is not urgent."

"My wife and I have been discussing possible names for our daughter, and I feel I cannot be sufficiently confident about our choice without seeking Lady de Bourgh's opinion on the subject. She always has the most insightful comments and ways of looking at a matter. I would be remiss if I failed to seek her counsel on such an important topic."

Anne hesitated, clearly torn as to what would be the correct course of action to take. Her mother would no doubt be very interested in being a part of the process of choosing a name for the child, but she was not sure it was a sufficient reason to wake her mother in the very early parts of the morning, especially after a late night.

"Perhaps it would be best if you delayed your decision for a few hours until my mother has come down to breakfast. I am sure that a few hours of contemplation will only aid your decision making process. My mother would no doubt give you the same advice if she was here to share it with you. You will recall how often she has told you to think carefully on a matter before making a decision, and how often a good night's rest can make all the difference in the morning. I am sure you and your wife could benefit from a few hours of rest right now." She looked around the room. "In fact, I think we all could."

Richard was inclined to agree. It had been a long night, and despite the tea and coffee, he was ready to tumble into bed for a few hours of sleep. He needed the time away from Gyles and Anne to settle his thoughts about their relationship and get this jealousy under control.

Mr. Collins frowned. "I do not wish to disturb Lady de Bourgh, and she *has* often counseled me on the wisdom of giving a subject sufficient thought. I believe your suggestion holds merit."

Anne breathed a sigh of relief. "I am glad to hear that." The long case clock in the room chose that moment to ring the hour with five long tolls.

Richard grimaced. Even with a few hours before breakfast was served and Lady Catherine would reappear, it was not much time to rest. He shoved himself to his feet. "Since that has been decided, I think it is past time I took myself off to bed. I suggest that the rest of you do the same. Can I escort you upstairs, Cousin?" He could not resist making the request. After sharing her for the better part of the night, he was desperate to have her to himself for a few minutes. Familial loyalty was a good enough excuse.

Anne was grateful for his offer. She rose gracefully and said good night to their guests, graciously declining Gyles' offer to accompany them.

Her mother might have insisted that Gyles' room be on the family floor, but thankfully it was at the opposite end of the house from her bedchamber. She did not need the man invading that sanctuary, too.

He was already much too comfortable trying to control her. She was not entirely sure what her mother had been thinking inviting him here. Still, she could not be rude. She had to give him the opportunity her mother requested, even if she was fairly certain her idea of a future did not coincide with his.

Once they were outside the parlor door, Anne wound her arm through Richard's and leaned her head on his shoulder. She was so very tired. It was emotionally draining to be constantly mediating disagreements and trying to keep her exhausted mind concentrating on whatever conversation was going on around her. In the past few hours, she had gradually resorted to mainly smiling and nodding as Gyles went on and on. She did not have the mental energy to contribute to any topic, much less one as mundane as his preference for shoes over boots. What sort of man even worried about such a thing? One with too much time on his hands, she thought.

Richard chuckled and patted her hand. "Tired?"

"Mm hmm," she mumbled, wishing she could close her eyes right then and go to sleep. Richard's shoulder would surely suffice as a comfortable pillow.

They climbed the stairs in silent tandem. Richard paused in the hallway outside her door. "Anne?"

She turned to face him, but her mind was already inside the room in her bed. "Yes?"

He hesitated. Now was not the time to ask her what she thought of Gyles. He could tell from the way her eyes drifted to the door that she was long past due for bed. It was not the time for serious questions.

He smiled at her instead. "Never mind. I shall see you in a few hours." Without thinking, he leaned forward and pressed a chaste kiss to her forehead. "Good night."

She gave a happy sigh of contentment at his touch and then reached for the doorknob. "Good night, Richard." She closed the door behind her with a soft click.

Richard stood there for several minutes, just contemplating the door that stood between them. Then he turned around and paced down the hall to the flight of stairs that would take him to his room in the tower. Anne might have given him the best room in the house, but it would certainly feel lonely tonight.

CHAPTER SIX

The noise just would not stop.

Anne buried her head under her pillow and prayed for the crying to cease. There was no such miracle. Mr. and Mrs. Collins' new daughter had a set of lungs on her that rivaled Lady Catherine.

Anne was sure that Mrs. Collins had done all in her power to silence her daughter, but nothing had been effective in the last twenty minutes. There was little use trying to return to sleep at this point. The three hours or so she had managed would have to suffice for the time being.

"Where is that child? I cannot stand this racket in my household! I demand something be done!" Lady Catherine's strident voice echoed down the hall.

Now Anne *really* could not stay in bed. She released her hold on the pillow clamped over her ears and threw back the covers. It did not matter that her maid would not be upstairs for another twenty minutes to help her dress. With the sort of commotion her mother was causing in the hall, the whole household would be up within minutes if they were not already. She needed to be available to run interference if necessary.

A quick glance in her wardrobe and she selected a simple morning gown that she would be able to get into without help. It was no peach silk; her mother would probably not approve of her selection if Gyles saw her in it. Still, it could not be helped. Already she could hear footsteps in the hall as one of the maids hurried to help try to calm the baby.

It would probably do little good, and if Anne knew her mother, Lady Catherine would find it incumbent upon her to visit the new parents herself if the noise did not cease quickly.

Anne threw the dress on over her shift, then ran a brush through her hair. She quickly braided the locks, then twisted them up on her head. It was a simple hairstyle that did not do her dainty features justice, but it did not matter. If Gyles Bellingham found her unattractive clad in her simple manner, so be it. She had worked too hard, sacrificed too much, to preserve the peace at Rosings to allow it to be shattered so quickly.

Down the hall, she heard her mother's door thrown open with a bang. She flinched as the harsh noise rang out, signally to any and all within earshot that Lady Catherine was not pleased. The servants would be fleeing for the lower floors at that sound. If she was smart she would be following them. It would be easy to slip out the kitchen door…she sighed and admitted the folly in that plan. If she slipped away, she would just have to deal with the mayhem when she returned and her mother's indignation at her disappearance to boot. No, it was better to stay in control of what she could of the outcome.

She glanced at herself one last time in the looking glass and decided she was satisfied with her appearance. She might not see the elegance of last night reflected back at her, but she was no dowdy pumpkin either. It would do.

Her mother's steps thundered by her bedroom door, rousing her to action. She quickly opened her door and stepped into the hall, just in time to see her mother's back disappear into the Collins' bedchamber.

Groaning, Anne followed her. She knocked lightly on the door, but there was no way anyone heard her.

Inside, Lady Catherine demanded loudly, "Hand me that child!"

Anne did not wait for someone to answer her summons. She opened the door and went in, much like her mother had. She winced as she crossed the threshold. If she had thought the din was bad in the hall, it was nothing compared to the level of noise inside the room. She was just in time to see an exasperated Mrs. Collins hand over her shrieking bundle to Lady Catherine.

The noise ceased instantly. Anne was shocked to see the transformation in her mother as she smiled down at the little girl and cooed, "Now, that is a good little girl. I knew you just needed a little coercing to settle down."

Still holding the baby, Lady Catherine settled into the rocking chair and set it to rocking back and forth. She glanced at the parents. "All this little one needs is a firm hand. I expect you will give it to her after this."

Mrs. Collins, who looked exhausted, simply nodded. She was ready to drop at any moment. Mr. Collins scurried over to peer over Lady Catherine's shoulder at his daughter. "I am so pleased to see her responding to you, Lady de Bourgh. It is my fondest wish that you shall be as dear to her heart as you are to mine, a sort of grandmother to her as my wife's family is so far away." He glanced nervously at his wife. "In fact, my wife and I wished to ask a very great favor of you."

Lady Catherine looked up sharply. "What is it?" She narrowed her eyes suspiciously at Mr. Collins.

He floundered for a moment, having not expected that reaction, and then pulled himself up to his full yet still insignificant height. "My wife and I would very much like to name our daughter Catherine, after you. It is a fine, strong, elegant name, much like your ladyship, and we hope our daughter can live up to the fine example you have set for her. However, I do not wish to be presumptuous. If you do not wish it, we shall look elsewhere for a name, although I know we cannot find one finer."

Lady Catherine's eyes softened. She looked down at the now sleeping child she held in her arms. "It is a fine name, Mr. Collins. This favor you ask is really no favor at all. I would be honored to share my name with your daughter."

Anne swallowed her squeak of surprise, but some sort of noise must have escaped, for her mother turned to look at her. It was the first time anyone in the room had acknowledged her presence, although in poor Mrs. Collins defense, she had promptly nodded off after handing over her child.

Her mother smiled at her and held out her hand for her to take. "Anne, child, you will not mind, will you? If you should have a child it will very likely be named after Gyles' side of the family. Surely, you will not begrudge an old woman like me this one small pleasure."

Anne shelved her protest at being linked to Gyles in front of Mr. Collins and squeezed her mother's hand. The parson really was an insufferable gossip and she would be as good as married in the eyes of the villagers by nightfall, but it was not the time to point that out. Hopefully, his new daughter would keep him closer to home for at least a few days. "Of course not, Mother. I think it is a perfectly lovely idea."

She did not know what to do with this new, softer side of her mother. She had never seen her like this. Was this the sort of grandmother she would be if Anne ever did have children? What a very different sort of mother she had been. Still, Anne had always known she cared, even though it had been suffocating at times to be under her mother's thumb. Mr. Collins had been correct to state that her familial loyalty was not be underestimated.

If Anne was not mistaken, she had just adopted the tiny little girl she held into that circle of family. It was too early to tell if the child would appreciate her future interference. Of one thing Anne was certain- Mr. Collins would be overjoyed to have Lady Catherine's input on anything and everything related to his daughter. He had certainly invited it by naming her after his patroness.

Mr. Collins beamed. "It is settled, then. Our daughter shall be named Catherine Francis Collins."

"A fine name," Lady Catherine complimented him, which only made him puff up all the more. Since the child had long since fallen asleep as the adults spoke, Lady Catherine rose smoothly and handed the babe off to a waiting maid. "Mr. Collins, I shall expect to see you this afternoon in my study for a lesson on childcare." He agreed eagerly and Lady Catherine turned her attention to her daughter. "Anne, I would like you to attend me in the blue salon. I have a matter I wish to discuss with you."

Confused and at a loss as to what her mother could wish to speak with her about, Anne agreed. Lady Catherine paused to give a few final instructions to the maid now caring for the baby, then swept out of the room. She seemed to assume that Anne would follow, and she was not wrong.

She headed straight for the blue salon with Anne in tow. She did not waver, which Anne found a little disconcerting.

The blue salon was not one of her mother's favorite rooms in the house, due to its less ornate styling, but with so many people in the house, she must have chosen it for its out of the way location. They were unlikely to be disturbed there. That knowledge did little to reassure Anne. She was used to her mother's strident demands, not this simmering restraint. Whatever she wanted to discuss, she must think it was serious enough not to be discussed in front of their guests.

Her mother seated herself in the precise center of the large blue velvet settee that dominated the furnishings. There could be little doubt she wanted to dominate the conversation as well. She had seated herself for maximum impact, so she could look down the length of her nose at Anne from her higher position.

Anne chose her seat with equal care. She did not have many choices, since her mother had made it plain that she did not plan to have Anne share the settee with her. That left her with a short bench positioned parallel to the settee, or a pair of armchairs perpendicular to it. There was no other chair in the room that would put her on an even plane with her mother, but neither would she take the lowest seat in the room, which her mother obviously meant for her to take.

She chose the arm chair farthest away from her mother. It was best to be out of striking distance. Lady Catherine would never raise her hand to her daughter, but she had been known to rap her knuckles with her fan when she was particularly irritated. Lady Catherine frowned at her choice, but she did not insist that she sit elsewhere, which Anne was grateful for. This conversation did not need to be anymore awkward than it already was.

Lady Catherine folded her hands primly in her lap and cleared her throat, signaling she was ready to begin talking.

Anne mimicked her mother's posture, straightening her spine and placing her hands in her lap. Her mother would expect nothing less than her undivided attention, so that was what she gave her.

When Lady Catherine was satisfied that Anne was paying attention, she began, "My dear girl, your attention to your cousin does you great justice. I cannot help but appreciate your familial affection and loyalty. We owe Richard a great deal for attending us this year and watching over our estate matters. However, I fear you have allowed your affection for your cousin to monopolize the time and attention you should be reserving for Mr. Bellingham. Since he has been here, you have barely spent any time in his company, and none at all without the presence of Richard or Mr. Collins. You must allow the man to court you properly! If you are spending all your time with Richard, it is simply impossible for Mr. Bellingham to fall in love with you. I expect a proposal from Mr. Bellingham before his time here is done, and I will not have you thwarting my plans." She thumped her cane against the floor for emphasis.

Anne fought the urge to laugh at her mother's accusation. Gyles Bellingham had not even been there a day. She could hardly expect him to be falling in love with her already. She might have been distracted by Richard, true, but he had needed her help. She could hardly have denied him that. In addition, she could not have foreseen that Mrs. Collins' baby would make an abrupt appearance that would forestall any time Anne might have had to spend with Mr. Bellingham.

Her mother could hardly blame her for all the unexpected events that had cropped up between Mr. Bellingham's arrival and now. Even with all that had happened, she had managed to spend much of the night in close quarters with the man. Granted, Richard and Mr. Collins had also been there, but given the circumstances, she thought she had done fairly well giving him her time and attention. Still, she could not very well tell her mother that. That was not the sort of answer Lady Catherine would appreciate.

She schooled her features into those of an obedient daughter. "I am sorry you feel I have been neglecting Mr. Bellingham, Mother. I shall endeavor to do better. I have no wish for him to feel neglected when he has gone to such trouble to visit us."

Lady Catherine harrumphed. "I am glad to hear you say that, young lady. I expect you to make every effort to make Mr. Bellingham feel welcome and to encourage him to make you an offer. If he asks you to accompany him on an outing, such as a walk or a ride, I insist that you accept. You must make the most of the time he is with us."

A frown creased Anne's forehead. "Yet, what of my duties to Richard? You know he has asked for my assistance with several matters already. You cannot expect me to neglect my duty to him, either."

"I do not ask that you neglect him, simply that you give Mr. Bellingham the priority he deserves. I am sure you can make time for your cousin in the mornings while Mr. Bellingham is resting. His mother has reassured me that while we are accustomed to country hours, he keeps city hours regardless of where he is. That should give you an opportunity to help Richard if he needs it. Truly, though, I expect he will get along just fine without you."

Anne did not bother trying to correct her mother. She had worked too hard to keep the extent of her involvement in the day-to-day running of the estate from her mother to let the secret out now. As far as her mother knew, Richard and Darcy had been running the estate for them for years.

She did not need to contradict that misunderstanding. It would just cause more trouble than it was worth. Instead, she promised, "I will do my best to make sure I accommodate both Mr. Bellingham and Richard. Mr. Bellingham's city hours should make that an easy enough proposition."

Her mother nodded, apparently satisfied that she had convinced her daughter to go along with her plan. "That is all I ask. I know your aunt and uncle and cousins think it unlikely you will ever be a bride, but I intend to prove them wrong. I will be a grandmother before I die."

Anne smiled a little to herself. She loved how her happiness was secondary to her mother's. Still, she would not fault her mother's motives, even if she did fault her methods. She truly was interested in a better life for her daughter. She just did not recognize that a better life did not necessarily mean a good match and matrimony.

Anne brushed off her skirts and stood. "I have enjoyed our little talk, Mother, but if you will excuse me, I wish to check on breakfast. We must make sure it is up to Mr. Bellingham's standards."

Lady Catherine nodded. "By all means, daughter. I am pleased to see you take an interest in his welfare. The way to a man's heart is through his stomach, after all. I believe I shall stay here for a while. I have a few letters I need to write."

She could just as easily have written her letters in her chambers or in the downstairs parlor, but Anne did not question her. Instead, she nodded and walked sedately from the room.

She did really need to check on breakfast. There was no way of knowing what her mother had ordered from Cook. Usually Anne was the one in charge of the budget and menu planning. With her mother suddenly exerting her authority, she needed to see what damage had been done and what she could do to remedy it, both with Cook in the kitchen and with the budget. Cook did not take well to her mother's orders, and she would be even less happy to have to accommodate Mr. Bellingham's city tastes and hours.

She met Richard in the hall on her way down. Her cousin looked about as harried and exhausted as she felt. She smiled at him. "Where are you off to at this time of the morning? I expected you to be sleeping in, like the rest of our guests."

"I do not know how anyone could sleep after all the racket this morning. I gave up trying, although the noise apparently did not deter your Mr. Bellingham."

He ran a hand through his already disheveled hair. She did not think his valet would approve of him roaming the halls in such a condition, but she rather appreciated his rumpled state. She could imagine that this was how he would appear first thing in the morning, the way only his wife and valet would see him. Her fingers itched with the urge to brush the hair that kept falling forward out of his eyes.

"The noise woke me up, too," she told him, forcing her gaze to remain steady on his. If she allowed her eyes to wander, her mind would too, to just how attractive she found him. "Where are you headed?"

"Out for a ride," he told her. "I need to ride some fences this morning to check for breaks in the walls. Your steward mentioned you have had some sheep go missing in the last few months. I want to make sure it is an isolated occurrence. Where one goes, others will follow."

"You do not think it is poachers, do you?" she asked, finally daring to voice the worry that had plagued her ever since the steward had mentioned the missing livestock to her.

He shook his head. "I think not. It would have become more of a persistent problem if that was the case. It is likely just a loose board or a section of stones that was knocked over that allowed the sheep to wander off. It does happen occasionally, especially if no one is riding the fences regularly."

"That is good to know," she said with obvious relief. "Come, I will walk you out. I need to speak with the cook about breakfast anyway."

Richard looked at her askance. "We are going to go through the kitchen?"

She chuckled. "It is the most direct route. That makes it the logical choice. Are you telling me you have never been in the kitchen of your family home?"

"Well, no," he admitted as he walked beside her down the hall. "As a child I used to sneak into the kitchen and ply Cook for sweets. She always kept a jar of cookies filled on the counter for us children."

Anne smiled. "I believe every cook worth their salt has a jar of cookies in the kitchen. Our cook still does, even though there has not been a child in this house in years. I was no different than you. The kitchen has always been one of the most welcoming rooms in this house for me. Cook used to let me sit at the counter and help her roll out pie crust. Some of my happiest memories are in that room. As I grew older it became less socially acceptable, even in her eyes, but I still go in and out through that entrance quite often. The servants pay me little mind, as long as I do not get in anyone's way. It will be no different for you."

"If you say so," he said. She could see he did not really doubt her. In fact, he seemed secretly delighted by the small act of disobedience. The rebel in him was showing, much as hers was.

She led him through the winding halls and down the stairs to the servants' level. Here the halls were darker, with little natural light, and she was forced to walk slower.

Richard slowed his pace to match hers. They stepped out of the way of a passing maid, loaded down with a bucket and rags. Richard was pleasantly surprised when she did not give them a second glance. It was just as Anne had said. He felt like he had discovered an entirely new part of the house. What fresh perspective could he gain from traversing these halls in the bowels of the house? This was certainly a different side of Rosings than he had ever seen before.

Would he be as welcome in their midst without Anne to pave the way for him? Rosings was not particularly known for its warm welcome, but he thought that had more to do with his aunt than the attitude of the servants.

He followed Anne into the kitchen, where she showed him the exterior door that would lead to the stables. He slipped outside, already missing her warm company, as she went to speak to the cook.

Sometime later, Anne emerged from the depths of the house, her mind still contemplating all the cook had shared with her. Her mother had blown the budget completely out of the water, ordering far more dishes and more expensive fare than usual, all for the sake of their guest. The good news was, Cook would be able to accommodate Mr. Bellingham's city tastes without too much maneuvering of what they had already planned for the week. The other piece of good news was that Anne knew from the ledgers she had gone over just the day before that the estate was doing well enough to cover the splurges. She just did not want a propensity toward excess to become her mother's habit. Economy, while not a trademark of the upper class, was a necessity if they wanted to live within their means.

She was still deep in thought when Gyles Bellingham hailed her from the doorway of the drawing room. She turned to face him with a start. "Oh! Pardon me, Mr. Bellingham. I did not see you standing there."

"I can see that," he told her with a jovial grin. "You were certainly deep in thought. What troubles could put a frown on your face this early in the morning?"

Anne did not bother to inform him she had already been up for hours. It was hardly early. She had gone to bed in the early hours of the morning. This was late morning, almost afternoon. "Oh, I simply had some household matters on my mind. You will be pleased to know that breakfast will be served in a quarter of an hour. Since we were all up so late awaiting the birth of Mr. and Mrs. Collins' daughter, the cook had the foresight to serve it later than usual."

"I always say that an early meal is bad for the digestion anyway," he told her. "My theory is that the stomach needs time to settle from the excesses of dinner the night before. Do you not find that you feel better if you eat later in the day?"

"On the contrary, I find that if I eat too late in the morning I begin to feel ill. I am glad the meal has not been pushed back any farther, for I would have had to find sustenance in the kitchens," Anne said.

Mr. Bellingham frowned at her and Anne quickly stepped away, forestalling any argument he might offer her. She was not in the mood to debate the merits of an early or late breakfast. "Well, I simply must see how Mr. and Mrs. Collins are getting along. The doctor was in to see them this morning and I wish to see what his prognosis is. Mr. Collins seemed to be under the impression he would insist Mrs. Collins and the babe stay at Rosings for a fortnight."

Gyles stepped forward to stall her, laying a hand on her arm. She glanced at it, disconcerted, and he pulled it away quickly. "Forgive me, Miss de Bourgh. I had a request I wished to make of you."

Her mother's request echoing in her mind, Anne responded, "Of course, Mr. Bellingham. If I can help in any way, please do not hesitate to ask."

He smiled wryly. "It is not so much what you can do for me, Miss de Bourgh, but what I can do for you. I simply wished to request the honor of taking you for a drive this afternoon. Your mother has told me how much you enjoy taking your little cart and pony out for a drive."

The prospect did not thrill her the way it might have only a few weeks ago. Back then, she would have been hungry for any male attention, wondering what it might hold for her. Now, she forced herself to smile and respond in a way her mother would deem appropriate. "Thank you, Mr. Bellingham. That sounds like a lovely idea. What time shall I be ready?"

She was surprised and a little amused to see relief cross his face. "Say about three o'clock? I shall wait for you in the parlor, if that is acceptable."

"That should not be a problem," she assured him. "I shall look forward to it." Awkwardly, she stepped back. "I really must go check on the Collins now. I shall see you at breakfast in a few minutes."

He nodded, stepping back into the drawing room so she could proceed. "Yes. Breakfast sounds good. I am looking forward to seeing what other delicacies your cook has managed to prepare. She is quite the expert."

Anne smiled. "I will tell her you said that. Cook always welcomes a compliment." Without saying more, she continued on, confused by the unexpected turn of events. It seemed Gyles Bellingham was fully invested in pursuing a courtship with her, despite their differences. She would have to do as she had promised her mother and give him the opportunity to woo her.

It was too bad, really, that any attraction she might have had to him was overshadowed by her attraction to Richard. When she placed the two men side by side, there was no comparison. Gyles was nowhere near the man Richard was. She could not help but wish it was her cousin who had asked her for a carriage ride.

Still, she was determined to give Mr. Bellingham a fair chance. It was the proper and right thing to do. If only she could convince her heart it was the best option, too.

She was still trying to convince herself of that when she met Mr. Bellingham in the parlor that afternoon, but she had more immediate worries. The beautiful blue sky of the morning had clouded over with a thick gray gravy. She looked out the window and worried. "Do you think we should go out? It looks like rain. Perhaps we should postpone our drive until tomorrow and entertain ourselves indoors. I have no wish for either you or me to become ill."

Gyles came to stand behind her at the window. "Nonsense. The day has gone a bit dreary, that is true. However, that is no reason to give up our fun and confine ourselves indoors. I have been looking forward to our drive all day. I shall not let a few clouds dissuade me."

She could see from the stubborn set of his jaw that there would be no convincing him otherwise, but she had to try. She protested, "My mother has often counseled me to stay indoors if the weather looks the least bit threatening. She is very concerned for my health, you know."

"Ah, but even you have admitted that your health is much improved. Surely, a little drive in the fresh spring air will do you well, not harm you. Even your mother has commented on the benefits of driving in your cart and pony," Gyles pointed out.

She could not dispute his logic, even though those clouds definitely looked like rain. She was torn between her mother's conflicting admonitions. She was to watch out for her health, yet she was to give Gyles her priority. With a sigh, she acquiesced. "As you wish. I do not wish to deprive you of a drive when I have promised you I shall."

He led the way outside and handed her up into the open carriage. A minute later, he had joined her and taken up the reins. He grinned widely at her as he set the horses to a trot. "You are going to have a wonderful time, I promise you that. You will not regret it. I have been told I am an excellent driver and companion."

Anne just smiled wanly and held on tight as the carriage moved swiftly away from the house.

*****

Richard paced by the drawing room window, watching the rain run rivulets down the windowpane. "They should have been back by now," he groused. "Why did he not turn back at the first sign of rain? He knows how precarious Anne's health is!"

Lady Catherine harrumphed. "Indeed. I cannot believe he can be so callous to my daughter's needs. I am sure she would have tried to prevent him from going out in this weather. Why, she told me over tea that she was worried about the turn the weather had taken! This does not speak very favorably of Mr. Bellingham. No, indeed! If Anne becomes ill, I shall find it very difficult to forgive this indiscretion."

Richard was inclined to agree. It just might be the first time he and Lady Catherine saw eye to eye on a matter. "He shall have a lot to answer for when they return." He caught a glimpse of movement out of the corner of his eye and turned to look out the window once again. A surge of relief filled him as he caught sight of Gyles and Anne, drenched to the skin.

He rushed out of the room to meet them at the door, calling over his shoulder, "They have returned. We are going to need towels, Aunt Catherine. Lots of towels." Given her concern for her daughter, he did not doubt she would see to it.

He made it to the front door as Anne and Gyles were coming through it. He was out of his jacket in a moment, wrapping the dry fabric around her trembling shoulders. The light gown she wore had done little to protect her from the elements.

She snuggled into the jacket, still warm from the heat of his body and smiled her thanks. It was too much effort to coax the words from her chattering teeth and trembling lips but Richard did not seem to expect any. He was too busy glaring at Gyles Bellingham.

He settled his arm over Anne's shoulders possessively and she sighed and snuggled into his warmth, not even caring that it could be considered unseemly. All she could think about at that moment was getting warm. She coughed delicately, trying to ignore the tickle in her throat. It was probably nothing.

Unfortunately, she could not hide the noise from Richard. He accused Gyles, "What were you thinking, going for a drive? Even I could tell that it was going to rain! It was unwise to go out. You have been warned that Anne has to take care with her health! How could you be so uncaring?!"

Gyles drew himself up straight. "Miss de Bourgh chose to go with me. I did not force her to go. We were having a lovely time until the rain started. I can hardly control the weather!"

Lady Catherine appeared in the hall at that moment, cane thumping loudly. A maid followed closely behind her with a stack of towels so high it almost obscured her vision. "I do not expect the impossible from you, Mr. Bellingham. None of us can control the weather. However, I do expect that you will treat my daughter with consideration. And just so we are clear, I do not consider dragging her out in the middle of a rainstorm to be considerate." She scowled at him and thumped her cane on the floor for emphasis.

The maid began handing out towels, and Anne started to shrug out of Richard's jacket only to have him stop her with a shake of his head. "Keep it. You will need it until we can get you upstairs and tucked into bed."

"But it will get ruined!" she protested.

He took in her flushed cheeks and soaked curls and said, "It is no matter. I have another. Keep it."

She did not protest further, as another wracking cough shook her frame. Fear like he had never seen it crossed Lady Catherine's face.

"Upstairs, Anne. We must get you out of these wet things and into bed," she commanded.

Anne obeyed meekly, allowing her mother to push her toward the stairs. The chills traveling through her body made it difficult to do anything else. She immediately missed the warmth of Richard's arm around her shoulders, but his scent in the jacket wrapped around her made the loss a little easier to bear.

Her mother tsked as they climbed the stairs, leaving the gentlemen behind them still glaring at each other. "I am very disappointed in that Mr. Bellingham! I expected better from him. I am not sure I can allow him to marry my only daughter if this is the way he treats you. Why if he dragged you out into every rainstorm, you could very well be dead before a year is out!"

Anne sighed. That reaction was perhaps a bit dramatic, but she could not help but agree with her mother that Mr.

Bellingham had not treated her with the consideration she would expect. She had been worried about the weather from the very beginning, and had twice suggested they turn around.

Each time, he had ignored her and kept going, insisting it was fine. Even once it had started sprinkling he had refused to turn around. It was not until the heavens had unleashed a torrential downpour that he had finally relented. If he insisted on driving in the rain now, what would he be like once they were married?

She shivered in the coat. "I wanted to come back to the house and he would not bring me. I do not think that speaks well of his character. I certainly did not feel like he respected my opinion."

Lady Catherine harrumphed. "I want to see you happy, Anne. As much as I want grandchildren and to see you with a family of your own, I do not believe you would be happy with Mr. Bellingham. I certainly am not pleased with his behavior today. Let us get you settled in bed. We shall discuss the future and what it might hold tomorrow. There has been enough excitement for one day between you and Mr. and Mrs. Collins."

"You are correct, of course," Anne admitted.

They entered her bedroom. She was happy to see the fire had been built up before she arrived. The heat from the roaring fire hit her in the face, bringing even more color into her already flushed cheeks. She gravitated straight for the fire, holding out her hands to warm them and then turning her backside to the heat.

Her light muslin gown had not been much protection from the weather. Hansen rushed forward, nightgown in hand. "Miss de Bourgh, let us get you out of that."

Since she was feeling increasingly ill, Anne let her mother and the maid help her out of her wet clothes and into the warm, dry nightgown. By the time they had her in her wrapper and tucked into bed, all she wanted to do was sleep. The heat from the fire that had been so welcome at first had morphed into a raging wildfire that threatened to consume her from the inside out.

She threw the covers off, only to have them quickly replaced. It was so hot. So very, very hot. "Please do not make me," she mumbled.

Lady Catherine and Hansen exchanged worried looks. Then Lady Catherine sucked in a deep breath. "Hansen, I think we must summon the good physician. I want to make sure my daughter has the best care from the outset."

Hansen nodded and said, "Yes, milady." She hurried from the room to see to it.

Lady Catherine watched her go, then slowly turned and walked over to her daughter's bedside. She pulled up a chair and settled into it, setting her cane on the floor beside her. She reached out a hand and stroked the dark hair off her daughter's forehead. It was already soaked with sweat from her fever. She murmured, "Rest, my dear. You will need all your strength."

She bowed her head and sighed. What had she done to Anne by bringing Mr. Bellingham into their lives?

CHAPTER SEVEN

Richard would have gladly kicked Gyles Bellingham out of Rosings without a second thought, but unfortunately, it was not his house.

He had to abide by Lady Catherine's wishes, and until she told him otherwise, he had to assume that Gyles was still welcome as a guest in her house. Still, he did not have to be happy about it. He folded his arms over his chest and narrowed his eyes at the other man. "I suppose you think this will endear you to Anne and Lady Catherine."

Gyles looked up from toweling off his hair in the front entry and frowned at Richard. He bowed awkwardly, "Excuse me, Richard. I really must get cleaned up." Stalking off without further comment, he left Richard to watch him go.

After he disappeared up the stairs, Richard sighed heavily and turned away. The rain running down the windows on either side of the front door did nothing to calm his temper. He could not believe that Gyles would have been so careless with Anne's health!

Anne was too precious to endanger like that. If her coughing and shivering when they had returned was any indication, she was on the verge of becoming ill. He only hoped that they had managed to catch it before it was too late.

For how long he stood there, worrying, he did not know. But suddenly Hansen, the lady's maid that had come to fetch Anne from the stables the day before, appeared in the hall.

She looked harried as she called for one of the footmen.

Richard stepped out of the alcove by the door and hailed her, "Hansen, what do you need? What news is there?"

Hansen did a double-take, startled by his abrupt appearance. She curtseyed hurriedly. "Mr. Fitzwilliam. Forgive me, I did not see you standing there. Lady de Bourgh has ordered that the doctor be brought round for Miss de Bourgh. I was trying to find one of the footmen to send off with the summons."

That was not good news. Not at all. His frown deepened, scaring her into stepping back a step. He quickly erased the expression, since he needed the information she could give him. He could not risk scaring her off. "Is Miss de Bourgh ill? What has happened?"

Hansen hesitated. Clearly she was preoccupied with sending for the doctor. Richard could not blame her, but he was desperate for any news of Anne.

Finally, she capitulated. "By the time we got Miss de Bourgh settled in bed, she was burning up with a fever. I am afraid she is talking out of her head. We must get the doctor up to the house."

Richard agreed. He let her go on her way without any further delay. Instead, he paced the halls, then decided he was better off upstairs, near Anne. The distance between them suddenly yawned wide and he could not stand it.

He headed upstairs before he could think better of it. He did not pause on the landing but turned into the hall and went straight to the door that led to Anne's bedroom. He knocked, fully expecting to be turned away, but he could do nothing else. His worries and fears would not dissipate until he saw Anne with his own two eyes. Even if she was in as bad shape as Hansen seemed to think, he needed the reassurance of being near her.

The reality could not be worse than his fears. He needed to see her. He wanted to be near her. He had to try.

Lady Catherine answered his knock. She looked haggard, more worn out and older than he had ever seen her. Surprisingly, she did not even question his presence. "Richard. Come in. I know you are as concerned for Anne as I am. Your devotion cannot be disputed."

She moved away from the door so he could come in. He stepped into Anne's suite and followed her through the main living area into the bedchamber. Lady Catherine moved slowly, her worry for her daughter weighing her down. Fear bowed her shoulders. His heart softened toward the old matron. He could not help but feel some affinity for her when they both felt so strongly about her daughter. His concerns mirrored hers.

As he stepped into the bedroom his eyes went straight to the bed, where Anne tossed and turned. He hardly noticed as Lady Catherine returned to her seat at the side of the bed. He went to the other side, crouching by the bed and taking Anne's hand in his. "Oh, Anne. What has he done to you?"

She groaned in her sleep and jerked away from him. Her rejection hurt more than he could say.

Lady Catherine studied him. "Pull up a chair, Richard. Do not take her tossing and turning personally. When she gets like this she does not know who is nearby, but it will comfort her to have a familiar voice. I have seen it time and time again, and this time it will be no different. You are important to her. Even I cannot deny that."

He nodded and went to retrieve a chair from the corner. He set it beside the bed and prepared to settle in for the long haul. He did not know how long it would take for Anne to be well again, but he knew he would be by her side until she was. She was too important to him.

A few days ago, he might have acted differently, but now, his world centered on her smile, her bent head over the ledgers, and her perfume in his nostrils as her elbow brushed against his. He could not imagine being at Rosings without her. She was what made this estate so special. Her touch smoothed the rough edges of her mother's handling, making the servants feel like their talents were appreciated and keeping the whole place running smoothly.

Even Mr. and Mrs. Collins benefited from her gentle care. He knew Mrs. Collins welcomed her visits to the parsonage and the voice of reason she presented around the dining table. More than once he had seen her send a basket of tidbits from Rosings' pantry down to the parsonage for their use. She was a wise woman. Anne might choose not to make waves in her household, but she certainly knew everything that happened within its gates.

She was direct, forthright, but she had a joy de vive that shone through regardless of the trials she endured. Without her, Rosings would have lost its shining jewel. She was the lamp that lit the household and restored it to its glory.

She was his light in the harbor, the light that drew him home. He knew suddenly that with Anne, he was home. There was no other place that he would rather be than with her.

It was probably a futile hope. He had no way of knowing if she felt the same way about him. Lady Catherine was determined that her future lay elsewhere, as Gyles Bellingham's wife. He could hardly guarantee her the comforts that she could have as Gyles' wife. His lifestyle was much simpler. Yet, he respected her and loved the woman she had become. He was not sure Gyles would grant her the same dignity.

Richard's feelings toward her were not those of a relative. She was more than his cousin. And now, he might never have the opportunity to tell her how he felt.

His heart squeezed at the possibility and he felt a hot surge of anger that Gyles had done this to her. No woman deserved such callous treatment, especially not his Anne. Never Anne.

She was too beautiful, too generous. She deserved the very best life could offer her. She deserved hope and joy, and the space to grow her roses and pursue her passions. She deserved so much more than he could offer her.

But before he could even start down that path, they had to get her well. Footsteps sounded in the outer living space, signaling the arrival of the good doctor. The poor man had been dragged up to Rosings more times than he could count in the past two days, yet here he was again, ready and willing to help. Richard had never felt such gratitude as he did when the man came through the door, bag in hand.

He stood back so the doctor could have access to Anne without Lady Catherine having to relinquish her seat. The physician conducted his examination in grave silence. By his few, pointed questions, it was evident that Anne had been afflicted with these same symptoms before. After he finished his examination, he held a whispered conversation with Lady Catherine. Their shared worry was evident in her etched features. Richard could tell they both felt that Anne's illness was serious.

Richard knew real fear. How could her condition have deteriorated so quickly? Just that morning she had been smiling and teasing him. This evening, she was burning up with a fever and fighting for every breath. The doctor left a tincture for her cough and ordered she be given as much fluid as they could get in her. He told them to keep the fire built up when she was chilled and bathe her face and body with cool rags when she was overheated. Other than that, all they could do was wait and hope for the best.

Richard and Lady Catherine spent the night at Anne's bedside. In the morning, when Anne was still no better, Lady Catherine quietly descended the stairs and held a private audience with Gyles Bellingham. Half an hour later, he packed his bags and departed.

Richard would never know exactly what his aunt had said to Gyles behind closed doors. Contrary to her usual behavior, there were no raised voices or slamming doors. She simply went about doing what needed to be done.

Richard was happy to see his competition go, but he would have been happier to have a healthy Anne, even if it meant he would have to see Gyles and her together as they pursued a courtship. He watched Gyles climb into his carriage with a heavy heart.

The sun shone brightly outside his window as Gyles pulled away, but the atmosphere inside Anne's room was very dismal indeed. The doctor returned that afternoon to check on her and the recovering Mrs. Collins, only to proclaim her no better than when he had seen her the day before.

The news spread a pallor over the household. The servants went about their duties quietly, speaking in hushed tones and fervent whispers. They stood about in little groups of two or three, watching and waiting for any sign that she was recovering. Richard did not bother to send them back to their duties as he might have when he passed them occasionally in the halls. They were as entitled to their worry as he was. Besides, it was nice to see that Anne was so genuinely cared for by those in her household. The cook sent up any little tidbits she thought might tempt their appetites and savory broth for Anne. The tray was almost always sent back down, the food that had been sent up still intact.

Mr. and Mrs. Collins kept mostly to their room as the days passed. At first, Mr. Collins had attempted to comfort Lady Catherine with platitudes and long monologues on the virtues of patience and endurance. However, when she made it clear that she had no use for his lengthy discourses at this time, he had retreated, leaving them in peace.

In other circumstances, Richard might have found the ingratiating man's fallen countenance amusing as Lady Catherine put him firmly in his place. Instead, it only served to reinforce the direness of his dear cousin's plight.

Even the new baby, Catherine Collins, seemed to sense the sobriety of the household, as she gave no sign of repeating her earlier squalling. The house was quiet, empty. It was as if all the life had gone out of it when Anne took to her bed.

It was a week before Anne showed any signs of improvement.

Her fever broke in the middle of the afternoon. They did not notice at first, as accustomed as they had become to no change in her. Her shivering and feverish mutterings had become almost common place. Hope had seemed just beyond their grasp and fading away quickly.

Richard rose from his seat to stretch his legs and back. The cramped position beside her bed was taking a toll on him. He took a step away from the bed before he noticed something was different. He cocked his head and frowned, trying to place what was missing. It hit him suddenly. She was not shivering any more. Afraid to hope, he touched her forehead with the back of his hand. It was cool to his skin. Feeling joy surge through him, he glanced up at Lady Catherine with a broad smile on his face. "Her fever has broken!"

"It has?" She put her hands on the arms of her chair and leaned forward to peer closely at her daughter. "It has!"

Richard reached for her shoulders to shake her awake, then thought better of it. As much as he wanted to see those gorgeous eyes open and look up at him in recognition, she probably needed the deep restful sleep she had fallen into with the departure of her fever. He decided to ask, "Should we wake her?"

Lady Catherine looked longingly at her daughter, but shook her head no. "As much as I would like to reassure myself she has truly returned to us, I fear the best thing we can do for her is to let her sleep. It is the only way she will fully heal." With a deep groan, his aunt leveraged herself out of her seat. "I am going to see what the kitchen has that might tempt her appetite when she awakens. I want them to be prepared."

Richard nodded and watched her go. Her steps were measured and heavy against the wooden floorboards, but the weight of the world no longer seemed to sit on her shoulders. She did not lean on her cane as much as it tapped against the floor. Her head was erect; her mind was focused on the task at hand.

It was good to have his aunt back. But it was better to have Anne back. His relief at having her out of danger was complete. Still, he could not deny the worry that surfaced in his mind after seeing her succumb to an illness.

His aunt had always maintained her fickle health was a reality, while Anne herself had seemed to dismiss her mother's anxiety as an overactive imagination. Which was the truth?

How would a future with him affect her health? Was she even strong enough to think about getting married and raising a family? Would bearing his children push her beyond the limits of her health? He would never be able to forgive himself if he lost her because of his own desire for a family, and he did not think Lady Catherine would either. She had already revealed her intolerance for those who jeopardized her daughter's health when she had shown Gyles Bellingham the door.

Could he bear to be the cause of her deteriorating health? It was not a question he could dismiss easily.

Even if he could resolve his fears about her, there were other, more practical matters that had to be considered. Where would they live? How would he provide for her?

Anne would someday inherit Rosings, but even in his short acquaintance with her, he knew she would never push her mother out of her role as head of the household before the older woman was ready to relinquish it. She preferred the peace of Rosings over the position.

His pride was another issue. He did not like the idea of providing for their family through Anne's inheritance. He wished he had some future to offer her, some way of caring for her, but with the selling of his commission, he was effectively out of a job.

True, he had funds to cover his expenses from making wise investments, but those were only enough to cover his needs, as few as they were. Setting up a household and taking on a wife would involve an outlay of funds he was not sure he could handle financially.

He would need the assistance of his family if he was to take Anne as his wife, either from her inheritance or from his parents. It was not a proposition he would make lightly.

His own pride demanded that he postpone it, even though the very thought brought him almost unbearable anguish.

However, his honor demanded that if he could not make Anne a proper husband, he could not make his feelings known to her. The last thing he wanted to do was make her an unwelcome proposal. If the depth of his feelings toward her was any indication, it would cause significantly more damage if he acknowledged the attraction that sparked between them than if he pretended it had never existed.

His mind was so busying enumerating his anxieties, he did not realize she had stirred.

Anne looked up at him from under hooded eyelids, wondering what had put that particular frown on Richard's face. She sighed wistfully. Even brooding he was handsome. It was too bad her mother was determined she should marry that obnoxious Mr. Bellingham. She really did not have the least interest in the man. He was practically a bully.

Richard, on the other hand, was everything a gentleman should be. Honorable, kind, jovial. He listened to her as if she was telling him the secrets of the universe and he did not want to miss a word.

It was not true, of course; she rarely had anything truly interesting to say. Yet, it did not matter. He seemed to think her most mundane thoughts to be important. She wished her mother could see how well suited they were…Her thoughts trailing off, she yawned widely. It really was unlike Richard to be in her bedroom.

Her mind cleared with a start and she stilled at the revelation. Richard was in her bedroom. Why was Richard in her bedroom? What had happened?

She knew Richard would not have made himself at home in her rooms without a good reason. Glancing around, she noticed the lateness of the hour and the roaring fire under the mantle. Richard was dressed differently than the last time she had seen him, and her mother was nowhere in sight. Some amount of time seemed to have passed since she had last woken.

Dread coiling in her stomach, she remembered waking up like this before. When she had been ill in the past, sometimes she would sleep for days, her mind running in frenzied circles and crazed mutterings. Was that what had happened this time? Had Richard been subjected to one of her spells?

She did not like the idea of him seeing her like that. Her health was her one weakness, her one folly. It had been ages since she had let something like this happen. She was always so careful. She knew her limits and stayed within them. She might not have the stamina that many women her age did, but as long as she did not strain herself too much, she was able to do just about anything she liked, and certainly anything that would be required of her as a gentlewoman. She could run a household and be a good wife to someone, but she was desperately afraid that after seeing her ill Richard would no longer be able to see the strong, capable side of her. Her mother had certainly forgotten about it over the years.

It was frustrating to be seen as weak when she was really anything but.

Her mounting anxiety made her clutch the covers to her chest and sit up, finally drawing Richard's attention from his ruminations.

His eyes widened. "You are awake."

His statement only served to confirm her fears that she had been out of it for several days. It would be difficult to overcome his impression of her now.

She frowned at him. "Yes. You seem surprised."

He seemed to flounder for a response before coming up with, "It is only that you have been ill for seven days. Your fever has just broken. I expected you to sleep for much longer still."

"Seven days?" She was flabbergasted. "Has it really been that long?" She had expected a day or two. That was pretty typical of the times she had fallen ill in the past. To learn she had lost an entire week…it was more than she could comprehend.

Richard nodded solemnly. "It has. We feared for your life. The doctor told us all we could do was wait and hope for the best. Your fever has only just now broken. Your mother went down to see about getting some food brought up for when you woke. I see it was not premature on her part."

Anne became aware of the rumbling in her stomach. She rubbed at the ache there. No, it was certainly not premature. She would welcome a meal to help regain her strength. Already her energy was waning. She sagged against the pillows, allowing them to prop up her weight. "Food sounds good."

"Nothing too heavy," he warned her. "You have not had a proper meal in a week. I am sure Cook would love to fill you up with delicacies meant to tempt you, but the doctor said broth and bread at first, with the occasional cup of tea."

She chuckled weakly at his protectiveness. "Yes, Colonel, sir."

He scowled at her teasing, but let himself be coaxed into a smile. "I am only looking out for your best interests."

"I know," she acknowledged. "I appreciate that. I have been in this position before, you know. I understand the costs of being ill."

"I do know that." He paused. He wanted to ask about her illnesses, but it really was not the time. He could not be quizzing her about the state of her health while she was recovering from an illness. He could not be that cruel.

Thankfully, Lady Catherine returned just then. She hesitated in the doorframe as she realized her daughter was awake and talking to Richard. "Anne?"

Anne gave her mother a wan smile. She could see how the worry over her health had aged her parent. Her mother always took any blow to her health seriously and personally. For some reason she always felt accountable for keeping Anne healthy, even though that task was beyond her control. Perhaps her mother just never wanted to admit she had to relinquish control. "Yes, Mother. Richard said you went to see about getting a tray sent up."

Lady Catherine cleared her throat and started forward again, cane clacking. "Indeed. I know you will need to regain your strength. The tray will be up momentarily. I only hope that your appetite will be up to par. Cook has been fretting for days and I am afraid she will overdo the portions. You eat like a bird under normal conditions. I always did say you would do better if you took in more sustenance. Still, the doctor did insist on light meals. I suppose we cannot ignore his recommendations for the time being."

"That is probably wise," Anne remarked, feeling her energy slipping away. Dealing with her mother always took more out of her than she expected. It was difficult to have to be the adult in most situations. Still, she could not deny that her mother cared. She would not be here if she did not.

Yawning, Anne asked, "What has Mr. Bellingham been doing while I was ill? And how is young Catherine Collins?"

Richard and Lady Catherine exchanged glances. Then Richard said slowly, "Catherine Collins has been surprisingly well mannered since you fell ill, and Mr. and Mrs. Collins have been very busy adjusting to life with their new child. The doctor insisted they be in residence for at least a fortnight, so we can expect to have them continue as guests for another week. After that, I suspect they will be ready to return to their own home. And as for Mr. Gyles Bellingham-"

"I sent him away," Lady Catherine broke in, sinking into her seat without preamble. "He endangered your health once. I would not risk him doing so again. He had to go. I cannot trust him."

Anne was shocked into a brief silence. Glancing at Richard, she asked, "But what about Mrs. Bellingham? Will she not be disappointed?"

Lady Catherine shrugged, one knobby shoulder rising and falling with nonchalance. "She will understand. She always did say that boy was too self-centered for his own good."

Anne's mouth fell open. "Mother! What a thing to say!"

"It is the truth." Lady Catherine was unapologetic. "I only wish I had taken her at her word. You might not have had to suffer so if I had been willing to see what was right in front of my face. That boy is trouble. His mother is going to have a hard time finding him a decent wife. You deserve better than to be treated with such disdain, and I could not abide his obnoxious attitude any longer anyway. He would not have fit in here at Rosings at all. Even the servants disliked him."

Anne hesitated, then asked, "What about your hopes, Mother? Have you given up on grandchildren?" It was difficult to ask such pointed questions in front of Richard, but she needed to know. Besides, he had already been privy to her embarrassment about the situation with Gyles Bellingham. It could hardly make the situation worse now.

Lady Catherine sighed wistfully. "It will come in its own time, I suppose. I was trying to push things along on my own timeframe, but look where that has gotten us. It has been nothing but disastrous, and now I have Mr. and Mrs. Collins in the downstairs guest chamber for another week. Mr. Collins may be an excellent parson, but he is not an excellent guest. I very much fear that allowing him such liberties in my household has gone straight to his head. Why just this morning I heard him ordering about Hansen! Can you imagine? What use does he have with a lady's maid? I shall be very pleased to show him back to his proper place."

"I am sure that if Mrs. Collins had heard him she would have set him in his place," Richard added. "It is unfortunate she is incapacitated at the moment."

Lady Catherine harrumphed. "It certainly is. That woman has a keen sense of right and wrong. She, at least, appreciates the privilege of being a guest here. She has not been the least bit demanding, just as is proper from a woman of her station."

Anne sagged against the pillows, relief making her weak. Her mother might finally be giving up on controlling her life. Still, her relief was short-lived. There was always the lurking possibility that Lady Catherine might change her mind and try to convince some other young man to marry her. Anne needed to work fast to get her mother on her side.

She stole another glance at her cousin. Maybe she could convince Lady Catherine that Richard was just the sort of man she needed as a husband. She was already convinced of his familial loyalty. Perhaps all she needed was the opportunity to see her nephew in a new light to see what a good match they could be.

Anne could not afford to give in to the yearning that yawned within her unless she knew she had her mother's approval. Her attraction to Richard was a living, growing reminder, but she would not wreck the simple life she had built for herself here without good reason. She needed to know if he felt the same way about her.

The fact that he had remained by her bedside throughout this ordeal spoke highly of his feelings being engaged. The awareness that had passed between them on other numerous occasions nearly convinced her. Yet, she needed to hear the words from his mouth. Without that solid evidence, she was afraid to move forward and see where this *thing* between them could go.

At the moment, however, she did not have the energy to try to convince anyone of anything. She just wanted to curl up into a ball and fall asleep. Putting together another coherent sentence was suddenly beyond her.

Lady Catherine noticed her growing fatigue. With a surprisingly tender touch, she reached out to tuck the covers around her. "Come now. That is enough talking for a while. I can see this news has taken you by surprise. We shall speak more on the matter another time. Why do you not rest until the tray arrives? Richard and I will step out into the sitting room so you may sleep in peace."

Richard opened his mouth to protest such an arrangement, but then quickly snapped it shut at Lady Catherine's quelling look. A glance at Anne told him her eyes were quickly sliding shut. She was, indeed, exhausted by their discussion, and she would no doubt sleep better with them out of the room. Following Lady Catherine's example, he hauled himself to his feet and followed her into the sitting room.

Once there, he went to stand by the fireplace, propping one elbow on the mantle as he watched the logs crackling and popping. His stomach growled, reminding him that he had skipped more than one meal in the last week. The tray on its way would be welcomed indeed, and not only by Anne.

Lady Catherine lowered herself gingerly into an arm chair nearby. She stared into the fire for a moment, then lifted her eyes to Richard. "I did right, did I not, by sending Mr. Bellingham away?"

It was an odd moment of vulnerability on her part. Lady Catherine did not second guess herself. To have her do so was a testament to her love for her daughter.

Richard felt his heart softening towards her a little more. His aunt was not simply a contrary, stubborn old woman with an inflated sense of her own self-worth. She was a devoted mother and caring parent. To the outside eye she would seem controlling, and in most respects she was, but she had the best of intentions while doing so.

Anne was not the only who had surprised him this trip. Her mother, too, was not the woman she seemed. How could he have missed so much on his previous visits? His own preconceived notions had blinded him to the truth of the matter.

Now, he was placed in the odd position of reassuring his aunt she had done the right thing. To be honest, it was rather uncomfortable and he was unsure how to go about doing it properly. He patted her hand awkwardly. "You did the right thing. Anne and Gyles Bellingham would never have suited. He is too selfish and she is too kind. Anne needs someone who will appreciate her strengths and weaknesses and look out for her best interests. Gyles is not that person."

Her gaze turned shrewd. "Who is the right person? Do you know, Richard?"

She was too astute by half. He had rather hoped his aunt had not noticed the way his gaze lingered on Anne whenever he thought she was not looking. It seemed that had been too much to expect. Even though she had been hoping for a match between Anne and Mr. Bellingham, she had noticed the chemistry sparking between them.

He wondered now if that odd moment of vulnerability had been planned, calculated to reveal his true feelings to her. Then he noticed the doubt and fear still lingering in Lady Catherine's eyes and decided he was not being manipulated like he thought.

She knew there was something between him and her daughter, but she was not quite sure of what it consisted. Her questions were designed to draw him out and reveal the nature of their relationship.

He was not quite ready to share with the mother what he had yet to discuss with the daughter. He hedged, "I am sure there is a gentleman out there who will see and appreciate Anne's wonderful qualities, Aunt Catherine. It is a shame she has not found him yet, but I would not give up. There are plenty of other available men in England."

He could tell she found his answer dissatisfactory from the way her mouth tightened and her lips thinned. She had obviously been hoping for more of a declaration from him when she gave him the opportunity. She harrumphed and thumped her cane once on the wood floor. "Lately, I have wondered if you are that man, Nephew. You admire my daughter. I can see that much. Her dowry would be a fine supplement to your coffers. You could have a secure future here at Rosings."

Richard refused to rise to the bait. Instead, he said firmly, "You cannot bribe me into marrying your daughter, Aunt Catherine. She deserves better than that."

His aunt wanted more from him than he was willing to give her at the moment. Things were too uncertain between him and Anne and his feelings too confused. He had to sort out his anxieties about a match between them before he could move forward the way Lady Catherine seemed to expect him to. Anne's future and safety were more important to him than giving his aunt the answer she wanted.

Lady Catherine wilted before his eyes, all the starch going out of her. "You are correct, Nephew. I have just vowed to Anne to let things play out as they will, and here I am again, trying to coerce them into working for me. I apologize for insulting you by alluding to your lack of fortune."

Richard almost did not believe his ears. He decided he could overlook her comment on his lack of fortune. It was enough to have those two other little words. Lady Catherine apologizing? Never would he have thought it! Yet, if it happened once, it could happen again. There might be hope for her relationship with Darcy after all.

"Your apology is accepted, Aunt Catherine," he said. "I understand that your motives were good. You are only trying to look out for Anne's best interests. However, it might be best to let Anne and I decide what those interests will involve."

A knock on the outer door forestalled any reply she might have made. Richard rose to let in Hansen with the dinner tray. She was all smiles as she set it down on a small table and uncovered the dishes. "How is Miss de Bourgh? The entire household is abuzz with the news that her fever has broken. We are so pleased that she is on the mend again!"

The maid's cheerful chatter was a welcome relief to the intense discussion that had come before it. Richard was glad to leave the subject of his relationship with Anne behind and quickly filled Hansen in on the progress Anne had made.

She was thrilled to learn that the young mistress had been awake and had even conversed with them. Lady

Catherine tired of her enthusiasm quickly, sending her in to assist Anne to sit up in bed so she could eat. While the maid was busy attending to her duties, Lady Catherine leveraged herself out of her chair and slowly made her way to the table to fill her plate with a sampling of the dishes that had been brought up.

Richard followed suit, feeling his appetite grow for the first time in a week. He took his plate to an armchair, not ready to set himself within striking distance of Lady Catherine's cane. His choice of seat would hopefully discourage conversation.

It worked. While they ate, Hansen reappeared, taking a covered dish from the tray that held a bowl of broth for Anne and some bread, and disappeared again into her bedroom. Richard would have liked to follow her in to keep Anne company while she ate, but with her mother watching him like a hawk he felt the risk was too great.

He would have to wait for a more suitable opportunity to speak with Anne. In the meantime, he had a great deal of pondering to do. When he finished his meal, he piled his used dishes back on the tray and excused himself from Lady Catherine, claiming fatigue.

It was not a lie. The last week of worrying had drained any reserves he had. He was tired, not only physically, but also emotionally and mentally. He needed a break from Lady Catherine's prying eyes and Mr. Collins' conciliatory speeches. Any outside influence was not welcome at the moment. He needed to be alone to figure out what he wanted to do about his future, and whether or not Anne could be a part of it.

With a heavy heart, he let himself out of Anne's room to seek his own.

CHAPTER EIGHT

Richard kept Anne company while she recovered over the next few days, but she could feel his distance.

It was almost as if he had built up a protective wall around himself to keep her out. She could not figure out what had happened between the time she had fallen ill and when she began to recover. He was gallant, charming, and witty; everything he had been before. Yet, something was missing. He avoided her eyes, and whenever she trod too close to a personal topic he quickly redirected the conversation. She was no closer to learning his true feelings about her than she had been while Gyles Bellingham was in residence.

At the end of the week, Mr. and Mrs. Collins departed for their own residence, and Richard dropped a blow of his own. As they sat in her sitting room playing cards, he told her conversationally, "I am leaving for London tomorrow."

Anne very nearly dropped her hand. She gaped at her cousin. "What do you mean, you are returning to London tomorrow?"

"Just that," he told her calmly. "I had only originally planned to stay a fortnight. With your illness, that was extended, but it is time I was heading home. You have everything well under control here. There is no need for me to stay to manage the estate."

"But…" She searched her mind for some valid excuse for his continued presence but could think of none. She had simply expected him to stay. Surely, there were no other pressing matters that would require his presence in London. There was no reason for him to leave. But there was also no reason for him to stay. Except that she wanted him to. She was not ready for him to go. However, she could not very well tell him that. She pulled out the one trump card she might be able to play. "You have not finished everything on Mother's list."

Richard laid down another card. "We both know that list came from you, not your mother."

Anne pressed her lips together and pretended to ponder her hand. "Well, I might have suggested it, but mother was the one who insisted I actually write it out and give it to you. It was the first time you had been here without Darcy. We did not want you to inadvertently forget anything."

"And you knew better than anyone what needed to be done," he said. "I understand, truly. However, there is nothing left on that list that you cannot do yourself. We both know you are more than capable of handling it once you are fully recovered."

She could not argue with him, but that did not fill the emptiness inside of her that had blossomed at his declaration that he was leaving. Rosings would be empty without him. She was not the only one who would miss his soothing presence there. However, she was the only one who would miss the sound of his voice greeting her in the morning and the brush of his elbow against hers as they sat side by side reviewing the ledgers.

How had he become such a big part of her life that she could not imagine it without him in it? She abandoned all pretense of trying to play the card game. She was tired of skirting the issue, and Richard had been the one person she thought she could be direct and honest with. She blurted out, "I really wish you would not go. I shall miss you."

Richard felt her words like a physical blow to his chest. Pain spiraled from his gut, overwhelming him and stealing the very air he needed to breathe. He did not want to leave her either. Just the thought of putting miles between them as he traveled to London filled him with misery. Yet, he knew it was better for Anne in the long run.

He had grown too attached to her. If he stayed, he was not sure he would be able to keep himself from offering for her, and that was the last thing she needed. Her recent bout with illness had shown him just how precarious her health truly was. He could not, no, he would not, jeopardize her life by asking her to be his wife and bear his children. It would take too great a toll on her.

He would not allow himself to think about what might have been between them. If he imagined a future with her, if he thought about what joy and happiness they might share, he might convince himself that a future between them was not impossible. Already he teetered on the edge of giving in. With a firm resolve born from his years in the military, he hardened his feelings. He had to do this. For Anne, and for himself. And he had to do it sooner rather than later. Every added moment in her company tested his resolve. Since she had already abandoned her cards, he set his aside, too. "I cannot stay, Anne. It is time for me to go. I shall miss you, too, but it is for the best."

Tears welled in her eyes. He could see the protest forming within her and knew he could not stay. Those tears would be his undoing. If they started flowing, he knew it would be beyond him to say no.

Leaving her was the hardest thing he would ever have to do.

He stood before her tears could fall and held out his hand to her. "Come, Anne, give me a hug good-bye. I shall be gone before you rise in the morning."

She took his hand and let him pull her to her feet. She buried her face into his shoulder to hide the tears that threatened as he drew her close. Richard allowed himself the one moment of folly, knowing he would never have another opportunity to hold her like this. He tipped his head to rest his temple against her silky locks and cradled her neck with one hand, letting his fingers dig into the thick tresses at the back of her head.

She was so beautiful. How was he ever going to bear not being able to see that gorgeous smile every morning? The scent that was uniquely her filled his nostrils. He nearly groaned. She was flooding his senses with her very essence. Then her shoulders shook beneath his fingers with silent tears and he could control himself no longer.

Sliding his hands around to cup her face, he tilted her chin up and lowered his lips to meet hers. She gasped as his mouth slid over hers. He had meant for the kiss to reassure and console her, but Richard quickly realized it was much more than that. He could taste the salt from her tears on her lips as they quivered beneath his. She kissed him back, tentative and innocent, but with a fervor that surprised him. It was as if she too realized this was to be the only moment they would have together. He did not want it to end and feared the moment he knew it must.

He poured his heart into that kiss, knowing there would never be another opportunity to tell her the way he felt, and hoping that she could feel his love in the intensity of his kiss. He could not give her the words, only this moment in time.

When they finally broke apart, they were both breathing heavily. Richard searched her face, trying to memorize every little feature for the lonely nights ahead. He wanted to always remember her like this, with her hair coming down and her gown rumpled and her heart in her eyes.

The urge to offer his heart to her was overwhelming and he knew he could stay no longer without jeopardizing her future. He stroked her cheek with his thumb and swallowed hard. "Good-bye, Anne."

He swooped in to steal one last tantalizing brush of her lips against his and then he left, not even daring to look back over his shoulder as he went through the door.

He was gone by evening. He did not even stay until the morning, as he had originally promised.

After that kiss, Anne had known he would not stay. He had given her his heart, but he could not give her his future. She stood beside the parlor window, half hidden behind the curtains, and watched as he rode Andronicus away.

All her hopes went with him.

*****

Andronicus was none too happy with him. Richard reined in his mount at the end of Rosings' drive and turned to look back down the tree-lined path. No one had followed him. No petite feminine figure ran after him to urge him to turn around and come back as he had half hoped she would. There was no one in sight. He had never felt as lonely as he did right then.

Andronicus craned his neck around to fix him with a cold stare.

Richard sighed. "I had to do it, old friend. There was no other choice. At least not one I could pursue with any honor."

The horse shook his head and whinnied loudly.

Richard patted his mount's neck. "I know you do not think we should be leaving. You made that abundantly clear when you tried to step on my foot while I was saddling up. I love her, too. But it is not what is best for her. You have to trust me on this."

Andronicus stamped his foot in protest, reminding Richard just how close he had been to getting grazed with that sharp hoof. It would have kept him at Rosings for several days at least. He knew the stallion had done it on purpose in an effort to keep him there. His horse seemed to be of the mindset that he belonged at Rosings with Anne.

"You did not even want to come here," he reminded the stallion. "You should be happy to leave."

His mount only snorted and turned his head away, effectively giving him the cold shoulder. Richard looked back once more, seeing Anne's tear-stained face in his mind's eye and remembering the feel of her lips beneath his.

This trip had changed him, in more ways than one. He did not need Andronicus' input to tell him that. He would never be the same as he had been before he came riding up this lane and encountered Anne, glorious in the spring sunshine. She had stolen his heart sometime between that first encounter and when she had fallen ill.

Her kiss had only sealed the feeling permanently.

London held no appeal, but he could not stay in Kent. He could only go forward and hope that time would heal the gaping hole where his heart had been, or at least numb the pain a little. He had heard during his time in the ranks that time healed all wounds, but he had a hard time believing it at the moment. The pain was too raw, too fresh. He could not imagine it ever dulling. He was not even sure he wanted it to fade away. If it did, what did that say about the depth of his feelings toward Anne? Would it trivialize the love and tenderness in their kiss?

He did not want to think about those possibilities. Instead, he turned back to the road ahead and urged Andronicus into a canter. Daylight was dwindling and he had to make it to the first inn before night fell.

*****

Anne threw herself into working with her rosebushes during the next few days. She could no longer bear to be cooped up inside the house without Richard to entertain her. Although it took some convincing, she managed to persuade her mother that it would not threaten her health. She was glad when she was finally free to flee to her personal retreat.

Lady Catherine watched her drive off in her little cart and pony from an upstairs window. She clucked her tongue and turned away from the window as her daughter disappeared from view. She glanced at the maid seated in the corner with some mending. "What happened, Hansen? I thought they were getting along so well."

"They were, milady. 'Tis probably simply a lover's quarrel. He will be back," the lady's maid reassured her.

Lady Catherine shook her head. "No. It is more than that. I have never seen Richard looking as grim as he was when Anne was ill. Before that the man was head over heels for her. All logic had flown out the window. Why, I was afraid he was going to engage in fisticuffs with Gyles Bellingham when he brought Anne back soaked to the bone! Something happened since then to change his mind, and now my daughter is unhappy. I must think of a way to fix this."

"As you wish, milady. Shall I call for paper and ink?" asked Hansen.

The older woman straightened in her seat. "Yes, Hansen. I think I shall write to my nephew and see what course he suggests."

Hansen hesitated by the door, confusion evident, and asked, "Your nephew? Has he not just left?"

"Not that nephew," Lady Catherine corrected her irritably. "I shall write to Mr. Darcy."

Hansen swallowed her shock and curtsied. "Yes, milady." She scurried from the room before any other questions could come pouring out of her mouth and jeopardize her position.

Lady Catherine returned to staring out the window. "Yes, indeed. Mr. Darcy shall know precisely how to handle Richard."

*****

Elizabeth Darcy hesitated in the doorway to Darcy's study. Her husband's dark head was bent over a ledger, his brow furrowed as he concentrated. Perhaps now was not the time to present him with the letter she clutched in her hand.

She pivoted on her heel to retreat just as he looked up from his paperwork and noticed her in the doorway. A bright smile lit his countenance. "Elizabeth. Please come in."

She could not refuse his invitation. She came to stand before his desk. "I did not mean to disturb you."

He said, "I do not mind. It was time I took a break from my work anyway. What was on your mind?"

She held out the letter to him. "This just came in the mail."

He took it curiously, turning it over to read the inscription. His gaze darkened as he recognized the bold handwriting. He thrust the envelope back at her. "Destroy this. I have no wish to know what she has to say."

Elizabeth ignored his outstretched hand and sat in one of the chairs on the other side of his desk. "Are you not the least bit curious? I know I am."

"Absolutely not," he bit out. "After what she said and did to you, I have no wish to have any further contact with my aunt."

"Perhaps she is writing to apologize for her actions," she suggested.

Darcy looked at her in disbelief. "I think not."

Elizabeth admitted that the possibility was slim. "Even if she is not writing to apologize, there must be some reason for her to initiate contact. Perhaps she is writing because Anne has gone into a decline or she needs your help for some other reason. If that is the case, could you in good conscience turn her away?"

Darcy set the letter down on his desk and fingered the seal. "I suppose that is a possibility. Anne's health has always been fragile."

"Open it and find out," she suggested. "Your cousin is an innocent party in all this. If she is suffering in some way, we are obligated to do something to try to help."

Darcy thought about it a moment longer, then reached for a letter opener to slice through the seal. He read quickly, scanning the contents of the letter. When he finished, he was frowning.

His wife watched him worriedly. "Well, what does she write? Is it Anne?"

He glanced up at her. "I...Yes. It is about Anne. And Richard." He turned the letter so she could see it. "Here, read it for yourself and tell me what you think, for I surely do not know what to make of it."

Brow puckering, she bent her head to read the letter. Darcy watched her expression closely, especially as she got to the end of the letter. When she looked up he prompted her, "So, what do you think?"

She tapped a finger against the desktop. "It is…most interesting. Give me a moment. I am still processing this information." She reread the last paragraph. Finally, she set aside the paper and folded her hands as she looked at her husband. "It seems to me that Lady Catherine is most distressed by this turn of events, and not simply for her own selfish reasons. She is genuinely pained by Anne's hurt and she seems to regret that Richard went off without making Anne an offer. It seems to me that genuine affection has sprung between the two of them. It is not unreasonable for you to act so that your cousins might be happy. At the very least, I do think it requires that you investigate further and see if things are really as Lady Catherine has said they are."

Darcy considered her words thoughtfully. "I believe you are correct. While I am leery of taking Lady Catherine's word for it, this matter does require further investigation." He smiled at his wife. "Love and marriage have brought me such happiness that I can hardly keep from recommending the state to my cousins as well."

Elizabeth returned his smile. "I shall pack for a trip to London at once."

CHAPTER NINE

Richard stared blankly at the four walls of his study. A full week had passed since his return to London, and he still had not been able to get Anne out of his mind. He did not see the dark wood paneling that covered the study walls. He did not even notice the pair of robins outside his window, building a nest for their young. He had been living in a state of comatose since his return, unaware and uncaring of anything that went on around him.

He went to and from his club, attended meetings with his solicitor, wrote the required letters to his family, and even attended a soiree. Yet, none of it seemed of any significance without Anne by his side.

He was going through life with no aim, no purpose, and he did not even care. The servants exchanged worried glances behind his back as he passed in the hall. His friends in the city expressed their concern that he was acting strange. Even his mother wrote that he did not sound like himself in his letters.

Richard knew it was the truth. He did not feel like himself. He was a shadow of the man he had been before he had departed for Rosings and Kent. Around Anne he had felt stronger, more like a true gentleman. Without her, he was nothing. He did not need anyone to tell him for him to be aware of the changes in himself.

He sighed and glanced down at the ledger filled with numbers in front of him. He was supposed to be adding the latest entries for the expenses of his family's London townhouse, but it held no appeal. In the space of a quarter hour, his mind had wandered back to Rosings three times. He wondered what Anne was doing at that moment. Surely she would be in her greenhouse at this hour of the day, puttering around among her roses. Or perhaps she had driven to the parsonage to check on Mrs. Collins and the new baby. He could see her now, with her head bent over the tiny one, a gentle smile on her face as she stroked the baby's soft cheek with a dainty finger...

He was startled away from his imaginings by a sharp rap on the door. He hurriedly picked up his pen as he called out, "Come in." It would not do to be caught daydreaming by the butler.

Only it was not the butler that came through the heavy oak door. It was Darcy.

Richard dropped his pen in surprise and came around the desk to clasp the other man's shoulder and give him a hearty hug. "Darcy! What a surprise! Now what could have pulled you away from Derbyshire and that lovely wife of yours? Have you gotten past the honeymoon phase already?"

Darcy smiled and patted him on the shoulder in return. "Not at all. Elizabeth came with me to London." He took the chair Richard indicated while his cousin resumed his seat behind his desk. "Strangely enough, you are the reason I am in London."

Richard raised his eyebrows in shock. "Me?"

Darcy nodded. "Yes. You and Aunt Catherine."

"Aunt Catherine?!" Richard closed his gaping jaw with a snap. "I thought you were not speaking to each other."

"We were not," Darcy admitted. "I had no intention of starting a correspondence with her. However, I recently received a letter from her that sparked my curiosity enough that I opened it and read it."

"Did she apologize?" Richard could hardly think of another reason Darcy might have considered responding to one of Lady Catherine's missives.

Darcy chuckled. "Hardly. You should know that would be too much to expect from Aunt Catherine."

Here at least was an expected response. Richard sat back in his seat, his curiosity still unabated, but his shock lessening. "Then what did she want with you, Cousin? And what does this have to do with me?" He frowned, his mind pondering the possibilities. "Does this have to do with Georgiana?"

Darcy shook his head. "No. Georgiana is doing well and really blossoming under Elizabeth's tutelage. I daresay she has picked up some of Elizabeth's spark, which, while not a bad thing, is definitely trying for an older brother at times." His smile at the thought of his sister faded away, replaced by a very serious look. "No, what Lady Catherine chose to write me about was your recent visit to Rosings. She seemed to think you left behind some unfinished business."

Richard straightened in his seat. "Is this about the list? I told Anne she was more than capable of finishing anything left on her own. She has been running that household without me for long enough to know what needs to be done." He fixed his cousin with a hard stare. "That would have been a nice thing to know before I went, by the way. It was quite a shock to find out once I got there. I very nearly bit Anne's head off for lying to me, when it was you who had neglected to fill me in."

Darcy grinned. "I imagine it was. Sorry. I forgot about that in all the hullabaloo surrounding the wedding. It did not really seem important at the time."

Richard agreed begrudgingly, "I imagine not. I have heard that love can make a man lose his mind. I see that you are no different."

Darcy glanced at him from under hooded eyes. "No, I am no different. Love does have a way of changing things, changing you. I do not regret it. It has made me a better man than I ever thought I could be. And Aunt Catherine made no mention of a list in her letter, although I imagine she would not take kindly to any task being left undone, even if Anne is fully capable of caring for it. She does not realize how much Anne does, you know. She has always seen her as weak and sickly, when the opposite is the truth."

Richard looked down at his folded hands. "She was ill while I was there. It is not a far-fetched assumption. She may be capable while she is healthy, but that good health is a fragile thing, indeed. One drive in the rain led to a week of fever and chills and talking out of her mind."

Darcy nodded. "Yes, our cousin has always had to be careful. I am not denying that. However, she does know her limitations, and she has been growing steadily stronger. I would not have entrusted her with so much responsibility around the estate if she had not been. It would have to have been a very strong incentive, indeed, to convince her a drive in the rain would be a worthwhile endeavor. Tell me, were you the culprit who suggested it?"

Richard recoiled. "Never! It was that fool, Gyles Bellingham!"

Darcy frowned. "Gyles Bellingham? Whatever was he doing in Kent?"

Richard leaned forward, brow furrowing. "Did Lady Catherine not tell you about his arrival in her letter?"

Darcy shook his head mutely.

Richard sighed and leaned back. "She does like to leave out the most pertinent information, especially when it puts her in a bad light or distracts from the outcome she wishes. She invited Gyles to Rosings in an effort to secure an alliance between him and Anne. She seems to be under the impression that she must have grandchildren, and soon. If I do not mistake my facts, she insisted Anne encourage Gyles by giving him her undivided attention. I believe the reason Anne agreed to go driving with Gyles was a misguided attempt to appease her mother. They clearly did not suit."

"Ah," said Darcy, with some understanding. "Just why did they not suit? It seems to me, they would be a good match. Their circumstances and family are well-suited. It would secure both of their futures financially. In Society's eyes, it is a match made in heaven."

"Anne needs someone who cares about her welfare, who is not always going on and on about his preferences with no care for hers. Gyles is very selfish, with no appreciation for Anne's inner, finer qualities. He enjoyed the thought of her as a jewel on his arm, but he did not look any deeper. She needs someone who will appreciate her passion for roses and encourage her independent spirit, not belittle it."

"Someone like you?" suggested Darcy, with a wicked gleam in his eye. He knew he had his cousin exactly where he wanted him.

Richard bit back his response. Yes, he wanted to say. Someone like him. But he could not have her. He did not deserve her. A match between them would not be looked on with the same favor as a match between Anne and

Gyles. He eyed Darcy warily. "What did Lady Catherine write to you about?"

Darcy smiled slowly, looking very satisfied. "She wrote that she believed an affection had sprung up between you and Anne, but that you had gone running off, leaving her daughter heartbroken. She desired that I return to London at once and convince you of the folly of your ways so you would return to Kent and make Anne an offer she could not refuse. It seems our aunt was not as far off the mark as I had initially anticipated."

Richard scowled. "I said nothing about an affection between Anne and me."

"You did not have to," Darcy told him. "I am a man in love, remember? I do not need to have the words to recognize a fellow brother in arms. You are just as smitten with Anne as I am with Elizabeth. The difference is, I am married and you are not. It is a situation easily remedied, I think."

Richard sighed, giving up all pretense. It was foolish to try to fool Darcy. The man was right. He was in love. "It is not as simple as you make it out to be. You have ten thousand pounds a year. Elizabeth would have had to have been a fool to turn you down."

"And yet she did, if you recall," Darcy pointed out. "At least you are not hampered by ridiculous in-laws that are bound to embarrass you upon every social occasion." Then he paused, "Well, perhaps you would be. Lady Catherine does tend to be a bit ridiculous, despite her station." He straightened. "Still, you are being foolish. Money is not everything. Anne surely has enough for the both of you. I have seen the figures for her dowry and so have you. You need not let financial worries be an impediment to a match between you."

Richard replied, "Anne's dowry is one of the reasons a match between us would be unwise. I have nothing to offer her except a small pittance of my own. I have no house, no property. Where would we live? It would be impossible."

Darcy frowned at him. "Do not fall into the same trap I almost did by allowing your pride to become a crutch. Those things do not matter to Anne, and you know it. They should not matter to you. It is silly to let such a small thing come between you. If I had let my pride keep me from marrying Elizabeth I would be missing out on the greatest happiness life has to give. Just as you are right now by rejecting Anne."

Richard nodded, accepting the warning he offered. "It is not only my pride that keeps me from proposing marriage. After seeing Anne suffer through that illness, it makes me worry about the future. How would she handle bearing a child? I could not bear to lose her like that. You know how difficult it was when your mother died bearing Georgiana. Your father never recovered. I would never be the same if something happened to Anne."

"Childbirth is always a risk," Darcy answered seriously. "My mother was in good health when she bore Georgiana, and yet she still perished. It is dangerous, and you cannot plan for or prevent what might happen. I cannot say I have not worried about the risks myself, now that Elizabeth and I are married. However, I would rather take that risk and have the wonderful memories of our life together than deprive myself and her of the joys our married life brings." He paused before delivering his fatal blow. "If you do not marry her, in all likelihood, Lady Catherine will find her a more suitable husband than Gyles Bellingham and have her producing an heir within a year. Will you be able to live with yourself if she does marry and die in childbirth regardless, knowing that you might have prevented it by your considerate care of her while she was expecting? Could you trust her care to another man?"

Richard refused to meet his eyes. He spread his hands on his desk. "I know what you are trying to do Darcy, but you must believe me when I tell you I have thought this through. I have no wish to see Anne harmed in any way. After the problems with Gyles, I truly do not believe that Lady Catherine will pursue such a relationship without careful consideration. I have no home to offer her, Darcy, and that is all there is to it. I will not propose to her if I have nothing to offer her."

Darcy folded his arms over his chest, displeased with his cousin's continued stubborn refusal to see logic. "Your family would not agree with you."

"My family has no knowledge of anything that has happened, and that is how it is going to stay," Richard said firmly.

"I would not be so sure of that," Darcy warned him. "If Lady Catherine found it incumbent upon her to write to me, while we are firmly estranged due to her treatment of Elizabeth, I find it far more likely that she would also have written to her beloved sister."

Richard tapped his finger on the tabletop, unable to deny that Darcy's assumption made sense. "My mother would have written to me to discuss any correspondence she might have received from Aunt Catherine."

"Perhaps," Darcy allowed. "However, if she has decided the letter warranted a trip to London, she would not have necessarily written to inform you of her impending arrival."

The suggestion made Richard uneasy, because he could not discount the possibility. His mother rarely traveled to and from their country estate to the London townhouse, but she had been known to make the trip when she deemed it worth the effort. He drummed his fingers rapidly. "My mother rarely travels to Town."

Darcy just raised his eyebrows, leaving Richard to bite his lip and look away. He knew he was snatching at air. Finally, he sighed and looked back at his cousin. "I will deal with that if and when it happens. In the meantime, nothing has changed, even if Aunt Catherine has written to my mother. The facts are the facts, and the situation is what it is. It would take a miracle or a calamity to change that, and I certainly do not wish a calamity on any of my family members, even if it does make choices like this easier."

"So that is your response," Darcy said haughtily, drawing his dignity around him like a shroud. He harrumphed. "I thought better of you than this, Richard."

Richard frowned at Darcy's superior air. "It is. You are wasting your time trying to convince me otherwise."

Darcy studied him briefly. Then he stood and made his bows. "I can see that my presence here is no longer necessary. I shall see myself out. I hope you will think over what I have said, Cousin. Marriage would suit you."

"Whether or not it would suit me is not the issue, Darcy. Still, I do promise to give what you have said some thought." Richard extended his hand to his cousin, not wishing to part on bad terms. Regardless of their differences of opinion on this topic, he truly did have the utmost respect for Darcy, and he would like to think the feeling was mutual.

Darcy took his hand and pumped it. "This will not be the last time you hear from me, I am sure. I have a few business meetings planned, but Elizabeth and I would like to have you over for dinner one night later in the week."

Richard nodded slowly. "Yes. I have no other plans. I should like to see how your new wife is handling her duties as Mrs. Darcy." He grinned. "And I have many stories from our childhood to share with her."

Darcy groaned good-naturedly. "They cannot be worse than the tales Georgiana has been telling her. I will have her send a note around with the details."

Richard agreed, "Very well. I shall look forward to it."

The cousins parted on good terms, with Darcy showing himself out. The journey to his own townhouse was short, and it was not long before he was standing in front of his wife, relating his encounter. He finished by saying, "So you can see, something must be done to get him to see reason."

"Well, just what do you propose to do?" asked Elizabeth, wise enough to know that her husband would already have a plan in place.

Darcy's smile spread slowly. "I am afraid our journeying is not quite over, my dear. We must go pay our respects to my aunt."

Elizabeth straightened in her seat. "You want to go see Lady Catherine?!"

He furrowed his brows at her. "No, not that aunt. Although I may not be able to avoid that outcome in the long run. No, I propose we visit Richard's parents. This seems to me to be a situation they would be keenly interested in."

Elizabeth did not disagree. "It would be a most beneficial alliance between the families. I cannot see why they would object to the match."

"I assure you, they would not," Darcy said. "The family's blessing is not what we need from this visit. We need to be able to show Richard just what he would bring to a marriage, and in order to do that, we need the assistance of my aunt and uncle. What do you say, my dear? Are you up to a little more traveling?"

Elizabeth chuckled. "Wherever you go, I shall go, too. I am always ready to follow where ever you lead."

Darcy smiled, pleased with her response. "Very well, I shall see about making the arrangements at once." He started to rise. "Oh, and you should probably speak with the housekeeper. I told Richard you would send him a note inviting him to dinner later in the week."

"How kind of you to ask my opinion," she teased. "Very well. I am sure we can accommodate you and your last minute dinner party plans. Are there any other surprises I should be expecting?"

Darcy shifted in his seat, appearing a bit chagrined. "We also may be expecting company when we return. I fully intend to bring my aunt and uncle back with us."

Elizabeth just shook her head. "I am glad I asked. Is there anything else you should like to tell me, such as plans to hold a festival in the backyard?"

"No. Nothing else at the moment," he said. "However, I am still formulating my plans, so be prepared for last minute changes."

She laughed. "It is a very good thing I love you so much."

Darcy just grinned. "It is a very good thing indeed." Then he rose to summon the butler and the carriage.

*****

Richard looked at his reflection in the mirror and grimaced. If his mother saw him looking like this she would be sure to inquire about his health. There were dark smudges under his eyes he could not hide after an endless number of sleepless nights. Those same eyes were red-rimmed and bloodshot. It seemed that all the color had drained from his skin, leaving him looking lifeless and lethargic. He felt lethargic, too. He had not been motivated to step outside the house since Darcy had visited him. He had not even been to his club to catch up on the latest news.

He had started losing his appetite about the same time he had started losing sleep, leaving his cheeks gaunt and his pants loose around his waist.

His valet had been clucking over him all evening as he helped him dress and get ready to go to Darcy's dinner party. Richard was grateful the invitation had specified that it was simply to be a family dinner, for he was not sure he would have been up to making polite conversation in a crowded room of warm bodies and pontiferous speeches. His brain still had not resumed normal working order, despite his separation from Anne. He could only hope it would eventually return and allow him to function as a normal person in society. He did not hold out much hope. Without Anne he was lost, just going through the motions as he tried to make it from day to day without much success.

He smoothed one hand over his cravat and sighed. His appearance was as good as it was going to get. His valet had done wonders with what he had to work with, but he knew it still was not enough to hide the devastation he felt at having to leave Anne. He took one more look at himself in the mirror and then turned away to head down the stairs and outside to the waiting carriage.

The trip to Darcy's London townhouse was short and quickly accomplished. Richard made his way up the stairs and through the door the butler held open for him.

He followed the sound of conversation into the parlor, where Darcy, Elizabeth, and Georgiana waited to greet him. Despite his misery, he was pleased to see his cousins and their smiling faces.

Georgiana immediately popped out of her seat and came over to give him a hug. "Richard! Brother said you were coming, but I did not dare to believe him. It has been ages since you were at Pemberley! When are you coming to visit? Do say it will be soon!"

Richard could not help but laugh at her enthusiasm. "I am sorry for the delay, Georgiana. Business has kept me in Town. But I promise I shall make an effort to plan a trip to Derbyshire, if your brother and his wife will have me."

Elizabeth smiled broadly and offered him her hand as he came over to greet her. "We shall be most pleased to have you. Georgiana sings your praises almost as often as she does her brother's."

"That is very great praise, indeed," said Richard good-naturedly. "For I know she thinks Darcy to be the best brother ever."

"He most certainly is," said Georgiana, with some satisfaction. "Have I told you about the pianoforte he bought for me at the townhouse? I am becoming quite proficient on it and Elizabeth has promised to play a duet if you ask."

Richard raised a brow. "Then I shall be sure to ask. I know how your brother loves to hear you both play."

Elizabeth laughed. "My intention with that statement, Georgiana, was to prevent a duet, not encourage it. I suppose I cannot bow out now."

"Absolutely not," Darcy said with a smile. "I have my heart set on hearing you play. It is one of my greatest joys."

The couple shared a tender smile. Richard cleared his throat and looked away, his heart aching for the sight of that smile on Anne's face. He had seen that tenderness in her eyes before, had known the joy of her smile. It was hard to be around a happy couple when he knew that the joy of marriage had been taken from him.

A movement in the doorway caught his eye. He turned his head to get a better view and froze.

His mother breezed into the room on his father's arm. "Richard, you look positively dreadful." She dropped her husband's arm to press a kiss to both of his cheeks.

Richard's mouth crooked up. "Thank you, Mother. I must say, this is a surprise. What brings you and Father to Town?"

"You," said she breezily. She turned to Darcy. "Are we going in to dinner now?"

Darcy nodded, fighting to hide his grin at catching Richard off guard. "We were simply waiting for your arrival."

"Wonderful," she beamed, clapping her hands. "I am purely famished!"

Richard managed to swallow his shock enough to offer Georgiana his arm. With Lord and Lady Matlock to usher them in, they all filed into the dining room and took their seats around the table.

Richard found his chair and looked around the table, trying to decipher what his parents were doing in London, and just what role Darcy had played in getting them there. His parents did not come to Town often, and certainly not unannounced. He was staying at their townhouse. At the very least, there should have been a letter informing the butler and housekeeper of their imminent arrival so that the house could be readied and their room prepared. There was no logical reason why they would not have gone straight there instead of to Darcy's townhouse, unless their sole purpose had been to catch him off guard.

He had to admit, he would not put it passed them.

His parents, as loving as they were, could be heavy handed in their children's affairs. Unfortunately, due to his somewhat straightened circumstances, Richard seemed to bear the brunt of their interest. He did not begrudge them their concern. After all, they had provided abundantly for him when he had been unable to do so himself, and he was still benefiting from their generosity by staying at their home.

He simply would have liked to have had some advance notice to prepare himself. And to figure out what their purpose for coming was.

He knew it had to involve Darcy in some way, for they had shown up here, at his house. There could be no other explanation, for they would not have come here of their own accord. And if Darcy had invited them… there was a good chance this had something to do with Anne.

Richard's hand tightened around his water glass as he took a hearty sip. His cousin was a meddling old fool of a man in love. He really could not blame the man. Darcy was in love and happy and he wanted everyone else around him to be in love and happy. It just so happened that Richard was the closest one and so he was determined to make it happen. He was a victim of his circumstances. However, what Darcy did not realize was what he wished for was impossible.

He would not call Darcy out on his bad behavior in the middle of his dinner party, but he made a mental note to take his cousin to task later, when they were in private. He usually did not mind Darcy's meddling ways, but he really had taken it too far this time. It was too much. Richard had trusted him with the truth about his feelings for Anne. He had no business spreading that information among his family, regardless of how well intentioned it was.

The white soup was brought out and the servants disappeared again, allowing the family to enjoy their first course in relative privacy and peace.

Richard's mother, Lady Matlock, took a sip of her soup, nodded her approval, and said, "So, Richard, dear, you are lately returned from Rosings. How is my sister?"

Richard could easily see where his mother was heading, but he played along, unable to avoid doing so without appearing rude. He concentrated on eating his soup and did not look up. "Aunt Catherine is well. She was busy doting on Mr. and Mrs. Collins' new daughter, Catherine, when I left. They had the foresight to name the child after her. Only time will tell if the girl grows up to view it as a blessing or a burden."

He hoped the mention of the new baby would distract his mother from her purpose. He had found a new baby to be an effective instrument to redirect conversations in the past. Women seemed to melt whenever a child was mentioned, and men were not far behind.

His mother brightened. "Ah! What a wonderful surprise! Catherine had not mentioned the child's arrival in her last letter. I am sure she must have been pleased to have Mr. and Mrs. Collins choose to name their child after her. She very nearly gave Anne her own name, you know. It was only Sir Lewis that managed to prevent it."

His father commented with a shake of his head, "Sir Lewis was the only voice of reason in that household. I am glad Anne took after him instead of her mother. It is too bad she has such a sickly and pale disposition."

Lady Matlock frowned. "Oh, yes. How was Anne? Has she improved at all? My sister always seems concerned, but that is her nature, you know. Last I saw Anne, she seemed to be doing rather well. She went on and on about some plants of hers of some variety or another. She had never shown an affinity for the things before then that I recall."

"They are roses," Richard said, with some irritation at his mother's dismissive attitude. Anne's roses were no small feat. They were something to be proud of. "She is breeding roses, and quite successfully. She has developed her own variety, or so she told me. I confess, I have little knowledge on the topic to discern for myself the differences."

"You could hardly be expected to," stated his mother. "No man could. You did not comment on her health."

Richard sighed. They had certainly moved on quickly from the baby conversation. It seemed he would be made to discuss Anne, regardless of his preference. "Her health is…volatile. When I first arrived, she seemed robust and in good health. She had good color and was quite active around Rosings. In fact, my first sight of her was as she was returning from a visit to Mrs. Collins. However, while I was there, she suffered a setback in her health and fell ill for over a week."

"Surely, there must have been some reason for her falling ill. What happened?" asked Elizabeth.

Richard swallowed. "She went for a drive and the weather took a turn for the worse. She returned drenched and immediately took ill."

Lady Matlock nodded sagely. "That will do it every time. You need not have poor health to expect that outcome from a drive in the rain. Why, just last summer I got caught out in a rainstorm and took ill for a fortnight!"

"Indeed," chimed in Elizabeth. "My dear sister, Jane, who has a most robust constitution, caught a cold after riding in the rain on her way to Netherfield. It worked quite in her favor at the time, which I believe was my mother's aim." She grinned at Darcy, who smiled back at her. Their tender gaze told him their memories of that time were fond. "I did, however, tell my mother she could not reasonably take credit for making it rain."

Lady Matlock smiled graciously. "Ah, yes, the infamous Mrs. Bennet. Richard did so delight in telling us about her. It seems your family made quite an impression, especially on my sister. I, on the other hand, have always maintained that you must have at least one relation that is determined to embarrass you. It keeps you humble. My sister Catherine is a fine example. I do look forward to meeting your mother in person, Elizabeth. I am sure she is a delight."

To Elizabeth's surprise, she really did mean it. Lady Matlock was nothing if not understanding. She had dealt with Lady Catherine since they were children, and she understood the value of seeing the humor in potentially embarrassing situations.

"Thank you," Elizabeth said, with genuine feeling. "My mother is not the easiest person to get along with, but I do love her."

Lady Matlock nodded and turned her attention back to Richard. "Now, young man, about Anne. A simple cold is not an indicator of her overall health. As both Elizabeth and I have demonstrated, that is a natural consequence of being exposed to the elements. You said she seemed well before then. I would suspect that is a more accurate indicator of her health."

Richard fiddled with his spoon, his appetite having disappeared along with his white soup. "I could not say."

"Hmmph." His mother frowned at him. She seemed about to say more, but just then the servants came back in to take out the soup and bring in the next course, offering Richard a welcome reprieve.

Lady Matlock waited patiently until they disappeared again. Then she spoke again, "It is disappointing that you did not spend more time with your cousin while you were in Rosings. I had hoped you would be able to give me a more accurate report of her health."

Richard went through the motions of picking out food from the dishes laid out over the table and piling them on his plate, even though he did not think he would be able to eat any of it. "I did spend a great deal of time with Anne.

We had much to discuss about the running of the estate. It is amazing how much she knows about what is going on behind the scenes."

He could not hide his heartfelt appreciation for Anne and all she did. He really was very proud of her, and it was impossible to hide the affection he had for her.

His mother picked up on it immediately, but she did not comment on it. "Anne has always been a very special young woman. Unfortunately, very few people have been able to see it. I am glad you are able to appreciate her finer qualities. Too often she has been overlooked in my sister's shadow. It is time she came out into the light a little."

Richard did not disagree. He picked up a forkful of roasted potatoes and stuffed them into his mouth so he could avoid responding.

Lady Matlock dropped her gaze to her plate and said carefully, "It is too bad she has not found a husband that appreciates her as you do. I do so worry that my sister will try to marry her off to a man that does not deserve her."

Darcy spoke up, "It is not an unfounded fear. Richard told me himself that Lady Catherine was trying to push Anne to pursue a courtship with Gyles Bellingham." He watched Richard carefully, looking for any reaction he might have.

Richard kept his gaze firmly focused on his food. He was nearing his breaking point. How many times would he have to rehash the whole ordeal with various members of his family? Surely, Darcy had already discussed the matter with his parents, or they would not be here. They were obviously trying to get some sort of confession from him. He was tired of these emotional highs and lows. He did not need to be reminded of what he had lost in Anne. He knew all too well what he was missing out on.

Every morning that he woke up without seeing her smiling face was torture. Every night he went to bed knowing that he would never again experience the joy of the sweet brush of her lips against his. He was miserable. And tired. Not just physically, although he was that, too. His sleep patterns had been disrupted beyond recognition. But more than that, he was emotionally and mentally exhausted. He wanted to be with Anne. He wanted to smell her sweet scent and be able to hold her whenever he wanted. He did not need to be reminded of that fact by all his varied relatives, especially not in the midst of a dinner party.

If he had known precisely what had been in store for him, he never would have accepted Darcy's invitation. He would have preferred to stay in and drown himself in the memories of the few weeks he had spent with Anne.

Those moments were going to have to last him a lifetime. Was it too much to ask that his family respect the barriers he had built around his heart? Was it ridiculous to think they could respect his wishes and leave him in peace?

He should have known better. It seemed everyone in his family had a control complex. They all wanted to have a say in his future, when all he wanted was to share that future with Anne. He was an adult, and so was Anne. He did not need his family to butt in with their opinions. What he needed was a way to give her the future he dreamed of for her.

Unfortunately, he could not. Even if his mother and Elizabeth were right about her falling ill being a natural consequence of being exposed to the weather, it still did not remove his inability to provide for her. If he could not give her a home, he could not be the husband she needed him to be.

Lady Matlock cleared her throat to bring Richard out of his thoughts and back to the conversation at hand. "Richard? Is what Darcy says true?"

Richard stabbed a potato with unnecessary violence. "He speaks truth. Lady Catherine had planned on marrying her to Gyles." He glanced at his mother, unable to hide his irritation as he added, "But I suspect you already knew that."

Lady Matlock set down her fork and rebuked him, "Really, Richard. That was unnecessary."

"Was it? Was it really?" he demanded. He shoved back from the table and stood, finished with this conversation and his overly meddlesome family. "I appreciate that your intentions are good, but I have had quite enough of all your interference. I truly wish Anne the very best life has to offer, but I am afraid it will not be with me." He gathered his dignity back around him and bowed stiffly. "Now, if you will excuse me, I really must be going." He strode out of the room before anyone could gather their composure enough to protest.

The rest of the family gaped at each other for a long moment, shocked into silence by his outburst. Then Lady Matlock picked up her fork again. "Well, I suppose we should have foreseen how that would end. He always did hate to be backed into a corner. It was one of the reasons he sold his commission. Too many orders he did not want to follow."

"However, he did not give you a chance to explain the reason for your visit," Elizabeth said. "If he had waited, the news would have been worth the discomfort."

"Yes," agreed Lord Matlock. "But perhaps it was unfair of us to catch him off guard like we did and band up on him. He clearly was uncomfortable. It would have been a better conversation to have with him in private. He does not yet realize there is hope to be had."

Lady Matlock nodded. "I agree. It is a conversation for another day. We shall have to sit him down tomorrow and have a good chat. It is not all bad though, Matlock; since Richard has left it gives us the perfect opportunity to catch up with our dearest nephew and his family." She smiled at Darcy, Elizabeth, and Georgiana. "How is life at Pemberley?"

CHAPTER TEN

Richard did his best to avoid his parents the next day. He went to his club. He took Andronicus for a nice long ride in the park. He met with his solicitor. When he returned, they were waiting for him in the parlor.

His mother smiled at him and patted a spot on the settee beside her. "Come, Richard. Sit down. Your father and I wish to speak with you."

Irritation surged within him, but he bit it back silently and obeyed, taking the seat she offered.

His father began by saying, "I realize we caught you off guard last night and we wish to apologize. It was wrong of us to try to force you into a conversation you were obviously uncomfortable having among polite company, even if it was all relatives. We did not come to London simply to make you uncomfortable. Darcy visited us in the countryside and relayed his concern that you were throwing away an opportunity for happiness because of stubborn pride."

Lady Matlock reached over to squeeze his hand. "First of all, we wanted to tell you that we would be more than pleased to have Anne as our daughter. She is a wonderful young woman that we have always admired, and particularly so as she has grown into her own. Secondly, we also wanted to tell you that we understand your misgivings about such a match. However, we do believe there is something we can do to alleviate your concern."

They must have seen his reservations, for his father added, "It is always a source of pride for a man to be able to offer his bride a home and source of income. I cannot find fault that you wish to provide for Anne. That is why your mother and I have arranged a wedding present for you. One of our country estates has been underperforming. Neither your brother nor I have the time or inclination to attend to it. However, your mother and I feel that between you and Anne, you could bring it back to its former glory. Your mother and I would like to give it to you, upon your marriage."

Richard was unable to answer for several minutes, he was so dumbfounded. Was this really happening? Cautiously optimistic, he asked, "Are there any conditions on your offer, besides the marriage part, of course?"

His mother shook her head. "No. You need not even take it over right away, if you prefer. I know my sister will find it difficult to give up her little girl, so if you need to ease into the transition, that is all well and good. It shall be waiting for you when you are ready to make the move. In the meantime, all your father and I ask is that you visit the estate once a year and review it, much as you have done for Lady Catherine and Anne all these years. I do not think that is too much to ask."

"No," mused Richard. "It is not much to ask at all." He felt a smile growing, warming his heart with hope for the first time since he left Rosings. "Thank you for the generous offer. That does make things a little easier. Now, if you will excuse me, there is someplace I really need to be." He stood and strode toward the door with purposeful strides.

His mother called after him, "Does that mean I am going to have a new daughter?"

He paused and cast her a warm grin over his shoulder. "If she will have me." Then he strode from the room and did not look back. He was headed for Kent in the morning and there was much to do in the meantime.

His parents exchanged glances as he disappeared into the hall. His father remarked, "That went better than I expected."

Lady Matlock smiled. "I knew it would. All he needed was a little push in the right direction and a little hope to hold on to. Much like another young man I knew not so long ago."

Lord Matlock laughed. "Still holding that over my head, are you? Well, milady, if you are going to bring up the past, then might I add that had I known then how conniving of a young miss you were, I might have withheld my proposal a little while longer."

She swatted his arm. "You always were a cad."

He grinned. "And proud of it." He stretched his legs out in front of him. "Now that we have our son back on the straight and narrow, do you suppose we can head home in the morning? I do find Town so tiresome."

She grinned widely. "Why, certainly, my dear. After I do a little shopping, of course."

He groaned good-naturedly. "Richard does not realize what he is getting himself into by acquiring a wife."

Lady Matlock shook her head at him. "Anne will be good for him, just as I have been good for you."

Lord Matlock agreed, "Indeed, she will. Marrying you was one of the best decisions I ever made, even if my pocketbook has suffered ever since."

They laughed together, then Lady Matlock patted her husband's arm and stood. "I am going to write a note to send round inviting Elizabeth and Georgiana to join me on my shopping trip in the morning. It is so nice having more women in this family. I cannot wait until Anne can join us. My sister does keep her so cloistered at Rosings. It is time for her to spread her wings a little." She glanced at the open doorway wistfully. "And for our boy to do the same. It is strange, is it not, how he is still our little boy even though he is a grown man about to become a husband?"

Her husband nodded. "Yes. We must remember, my dear, change is good. He will always be our son, but we must allow him to be a man. It is what we raised our boys to be."

She sighed. "I know, but it is not always easy." She brightened. "Still I will be gaining a daughter out of the mix, so I cannot be too disappointed. I do so look forward to helping to plan the wedding. I wonder what Elizabeth and Georgiana will have to say about the matter..." She wandered from the room, her mind quickly caught by a myriad wedding details that must be sorted.

Lord Matlock shook his head and looked about the empty room. In his mind's eye, it was twenty years ago. Richard and his brother tumbled on the floor, while his wife did needlework by the fire and he pretended to read the paper while surreptitiously watching her. How quickly those years had flown by! Still, the memories brought him great joy. He could not help but smile at the thought of Richard building such memories of his own.

Putting his memories to rest, Lord Matlock stood and went to find his son. Perhaps Richard would need some help packing if he was to be ready to leave in the morning.

*****

Richard rode Andronicus hard. He was eager to return to Anne, but he knew there was still one task he had to accomplish before he could ask her for her hand in marriage. He was not looking forward to it.

Under the usual circumstances, he would ask for her father's permission to marry her, but Anne's father had been gone a long time. That meant he had to discuss the matter with Lady Catherine. If her letter to Darcy was any indication, she should welcome a proposal from him. However, his aunt was anything but predictable. She had quickly thrown over Gyles Bellingham, even after proclaiming she was eager to see him and Anne wed.

The news of his parent's gift might also change her mind about pursuing a match between the families. A change of abode for Anne could mean even greater changes for Lady Catherine, and she really did not take change well, with the notable exception of when she was the one in control of the changes.

In the end, he knew Anne would have difficulty pursuing a relationship with him if it strained the relationship she already had in place with her mother. She had worked very hard to cultivate the balance she maintained between pleasing her mother, keeping the peace and being her own independent woman.

Andronicus seemed just as eager as Richard to return to Rosings. He caught his master's excitement as they neared the drive, picking up his pace as the tree lined avenue came into view.

Richard smiled at his stallion's anticipation. "That is it, old boy. Let us go to her!"

They cantered down the gravel drive, all but racing to the house as it rose up before them in all its majesty. As he reined in the stallion in front of the entrance, he looked up at the windows, hoping for a glimpse of Anne, but did not find her hiding behind any of the curtains.

He had not really expected to see her but he was still disappointed. If he knew her at all like he thought he did, she would be in her greenhouse, tending to her plants. It was her sanctuary. Considering how he had been managing these last few weeks without her, he had a feeling she had needed all the peace those plants could give her.

He hoped to rectify that as quickly as possible.

But first, he had to face Lady Catherine.

The butler who opened the door for him clearly had not been expecting him, but he was just as clearly very pleased to see him. He bowed as he took Richard's gloves and hat. "Mr. Fitzwilliam! What a pleasant surprise! Lady Catherine and Miss de Bourgh will be very pleased to see you. Will you be staying with us long?"

Richard smiled at the subtle inquiry. "I do hope so."

The butler fought a smile and pointed him in the direction of the drawing room, where Lady Catherine could be found.

She did not look up at his knock. "Hansen, I am not ready for tea just yet."

Richard chuckled. "I am glad to hear that, Aunt Catherine, for I do not quite fancy a cup at the moment."

His aunt looked up in shock. "Richard!"

He stepped into the room and sat across from her when it became apparent that she was not going to invite him in to take a seat. It was unusual to render Lady Catherine speechless. He had never taken her off guard before.

He folded his hands in front of him and leaned forward. "I wished to speak with you about a matter of some importance."

Lady Catherine managed to swallow her surprise enough to close her gaping mouth. She harrumphed. "Well, well. It seems Darcy received my letter after all. I was beginning to worry. It is good to know the man is good for something after all. That silly wife of his has not completely ruined him."

Richard ignored her jabs at Darcy. Her feelings toward his cousin and his new wife were beside the point. She was only doing her best to regain her composure. She would not have written to Darcy if she did not believe in the power of his influence. "Darcy did come to see me, but what I have to say really has nothing to do with him. This is about me and Anne."

Lady Catherine looked pleased. "I should certainly hope so! Have you finally come to your senses and decided to offer for her?"

"I should very much like to," he told her seriously. "Anne has become a very important part of my life and I do not know what I shall do without her if she turns me down. However, before I speak to Anne, I felt it necessary to speak to you about the matter."

Lady Catherine harrumphed. "As you should. As her mother, I have a great deal of influence over who she chooses as a marriage partner."

His aunt's impression of her own importance was a bit inflated, but never mind that. He had more important matters on his mind. "Yes. You are her mother, and so I wanted to ask your permission to request her hand in marriage. Would that be acceptable to you?"

"I should like that very much," Lady Catherine told him. "It has always been my wish to keep Rosings in the family. You have my permission to request her hand."

Richard breathed a sigh of relief at having that request granted. However, that was not the end of the matter. Lady Catherine might still change her mind when he informed her of his parents' very generous gift. "Thank you, Aunt Catherine. It means a great deal to me to have you say that."

She puckered her lips together. "I do not see why you should have ever doubted my acquiescence. You have always been welcome in my home and a very good nephew, who has done your best to look after Anne and me, unlike some other people. I see no reason to change my opinion of you now."

Richard fought the desire to shake his head and hid a smile. His aunt was irascible. "Anne deserves a fine husband. It would only be natural that you would want better for her than what I can offer her."

Lady Catherine folded her arms over her chest. "You will be a fine husband to Anne. I knew you were well-suited for each other when I saw your reaction to Gyles' treatment of her. I would rather have someone who will genuinely care for my daughter than someone who will be financially but not emotionally invested."

Richard nodded. "I appreciate that. I do have other news for you, as well. I may have sold my commission, but that does not mean I am without funds or options. My parents have offered me one of their properties, with the expectation that I will manage it for them. Anne and I would not have to move there immediately, but it would certainly provide us with an income and a home of our own when we are ready." He took a deep breath to steady his nerves. "How do you feel about that?"

Lady Catherine bit her lip, looking troubled. "My daughter's happiness is more important to me than my own, but it would be difficult to have her far away from me. I do not travel well anymore, as you know."

Richard could be compassionate. "I do understand. Perhaps we should leave that decision up to Anne, shall we? My parents have mentioned that as long as we are available to manage the property, they do not mind if we do not live there immediately."

Lady Catherine heaved a deep sigh. "I suppose that would be acceptable. I do wish for Anne to be happy. However, I would prefer to think she would be just as happy here at Rosings."

"She has certainly been happy here," Richard consoled her. He put his hands on his knees, ready to rise. "With your blessing, I would like to go speak with Anne now."

Lady Catherine raised her chin, forcing a smile. "Yes, my boy. You must go do that. We can discuss future options when you return with her acceptance."

Richard nodded. "Very well." He bid his aunt adieu and left the house to remount Andronicus, his heart considerably lighter. One woman down, one more to go. This next task was far more pleasant than speaking to his aunt.

He was impatient to see Anne.

He nudged Andronicus into motion, laughing as the stallion let out an eager whinny. "I know, old boy. I am looking forward to this just as much as you are."

CHAPTER ELEVEN

Anne snipped another errant branch from her rosebush. Her crossbred variety was thriving under her constant care and nurturing. The rose bushes had benefited from Richard's absence, even if she had not. She had done little else but devote herself to their care.

The list Richard had left undone still waited, languishing on her desk. She could not bring herself to finish what he had started. It was too painful to sit behind the desk she had shared with him and stare at pages filled with his neat notes. Her steward had hinted, once, that the month's bills needed reviewing, but had quickly backed off when she had burst into tears at the mention of Richard and fled the room. He had not brought it up since.

She knew she would have to face the books eventually, but she was not ready yet. In the back corner of her greenhouse, she took small comfort in her solitude and solace in her work, although even here memories of Richard beckoned to her. She smiled as she recalled his offer to help her, and the awkward way he had held her pruning shears as he had tried to snip off a branch.

The man was a genius on horseback, but he was helpless in the garden.

In the far corner of the greenhouse, with her back to the door and her head bent over her plants as her memories swirled, she was oblivious to Richard's presence as he entered the building.

Richard paused in the doorway for a moment to breathe in her beauty and calm the hope that bubbled within him. She was everything he remembered her to be, and yet so much more. Finally free to look upon her as a man in love, he admired the fall of her braid down her back, the gracefulness of her hands as she snipped. But there was more to admire than what graced the surface of his beloved. Under her pretty face and slim figure, there was a heart that demanded honesty and sincerity. There was a woman that made him look beyond his preconceived notions and take a second glance at the world.

She was light, she was motion, and she was the embodiment of purity and innocence. She was forthright and filled with laughter, happy despite the trials of life.

Although she was not happy now. He could see that much from the lack of a spring in her step as she moved from one plant to another. She was silent, when she might have been humming happily. Determined to rectify that as quickly as possible, he stepped forward. "Anne."

She jerked, pricking her finger on a thorn. With a gasp, she popped the injured digit in her mouth and spun to face him. He might have found the shock on her face to be humorous if he had been in any other situation. At the moment, all he wanted to do was replace the wariness spreading over her features with joy.

He did not blame her for being wary. At the same time, all he wanted to do was wrap his arms around her and assure her that all would be well. He extended his arms to her as he reached her side, but she stepped away, wrapping her arms around her stomach.

"Richard," she said, feeling numb. "What are you doing here?"

He tried not to let her reaction sting as he dropped his hands to his side. "There were a few things I left unfinished."

Her eyes clouded over and she hugged herself tighter. "You mean the list."

His mouth crooked up. "Yes, the list. I realized there was something you had left off it."

"I did?" She only seemed more confused.

"Yes." He dared to take a step closer, and this time she did not back away. Probably because he had pinned her against a work bench. "Would you like to know what it is?"

"I suppose so." She shrugged, feigning nonchalance and hoping he would not notice the way her heart pounded at his nearness. She had forgotten how potent his presence was. Already her heart yearned to reach out to him, but she did not dare. He was talking about lists and chores, not love and affection. He had not returned for her, as much as she might wish that was the case.

He took another step closer, then another, until his trousers brushed the hem of her dress. His humor faded away, replaced with seriousness. "Anne," he said, lifting a hand to cradle her cheek.

She put a hand to his chest and pushed him away gently, warning him, "Do not toy with me, Richard." Her handle on her emotions was very fragile, indeed. She did not have the strength to watch him leave twice.

He stood firm, refusing to let her push him away. "I am not here to toy with you."

Her heart wanted to leap with joy at his simple statement, but cool logic won out. That statement could mean anything. "Then why are you here?"

He refused to allow her coolness to dissuade him. He could not blame her for trying to protect her heart. He had done the same thing before he realized he had to step out of that protective box for a chance at happiness. Taking a deep breath, he dropped his hand from her cheek and took both of her hands in his. Slowly, he sank to one knee. Looking up at her, he said, "Anne de Bourgh, I have spent my life waiting for you. Will you do me the honor of becoming my wife?"

It was apparently the very last thing Anne had expected him to say, for she spent several long moments just gaping at him in shock. Just when he had about given up hope of an affirmative answer, she threw herself into his arms, laughing and crying at the same time. "Yes! A thousand times, yes!"

Richard caught her gladly, wrapping his arms around her and burying his face in her neck. "I love you, Anne."

"I love you, too."

Her whispered words made his heart sing. The moment could not have been more perfect. With a happy sigh, Anne sat back on her heels and reached up to caress his face. She cupped his cheeks as she laughed with joy. "Come now, Richard, that was not on the list."

"Ah, but, remember, I said you had left it off the list. So I was entirely justified in adding it myself." He fished the piece of paper she had originally given him out of his pocket and handed it to her. "Look at the bottom."

She did, her eyes falling upon the last entry, written in his bold, defined handwriting. *Tell Anne I love her.*

She folded it back up and handed it to him. "That may be one item you have checked off the list, but there are more you have left unfinished. Are you sticking around to make sure they get done?"

Richard chuckled, his arms still around her. "Is that your way of asking if I am going to be staying at Rosings for a while?"

She grinned. "Perhaps."

"Hmmm," he said eyeing her playfully. "Who is this coy mistress? Where is my direct, forthright Anne who does not beat around the bush?"

She laughed. "Very well. Are you staying at Rosings?"

He sobered. "Well, that very much depends upon you, my dear."

Her eyebrows arched in surprise. "It does?"

"Yes," he said, rising to his feet and helping her up in the process. He pulled out a bench for them to sit on and then picked up her hands in his again. Now that she was his, he never wanted to let go of her again. "I know Rosings has always been your home. However, my parents have offered us one of their country estates. So, you see, whether I stay or go really depends on you and what you desire. I shall happily stay by your side at whichever location you would like. Wherever you shall go, I shall go, too. What would you prefer, darling?"

She gazed at him very seriously. "Have you discussed this with my mother?"

He squeezed her hands. "I have. We spoke before I came down here to find you. She was saddened by the thought of you leaving, but she agreed to abide by your wishes should you choose to do so. She was rather remarkably agreeable, once I informed her I wished to offer for your hand."

Anne smiled. "I would imagine so, after all the hard work she has put into trying to marry me off." She sobered. "Still, change is very difficult for Mother. It will be quite enough for her to adjust to having me married. She is already used to having you around the house from your visits. I would not want to move away from her immediately. I do not want her to feel like she has lost me, when in truth she has gained a son-in-law. Perhaps, after a few years, when she has grown used to the idea, we may move to the country. I admit that the idea of a home of our own appeals to me." She glanced up at him from under her eyelashes shyly and blushed. "Perhaps once the children start coming."

Richard grinned. She was already thinking about children. "That sounds like a perfect plan of action to me, and I think your mother will definitely approve."

She peeked at him again. "It is settled, then."

"So it is." He lifted her chin with his finger so he could look directly into her eyes. "I guess that means I am going to be at Rosings for a good, long while."

Her gaze softened. "I am very glad you came back. It was not the same without you here. I was terribly lonely."

"I was lonely, too, and miserable. I never wish to be separated from you again. It was enough to have these few weeks apart. I do not think I would survive a longer separation. My valet was already lamenting the weight I had lost," Richard said, gesturing to his waistline.

Anne ran an appraising gaze over his trim figure and gave him a coquettish grin. "You do not look starved to me. On the contrary, you look quite well. Handsome, even."

Richard lifted a brow. "Really, my dear? You flatter me. I must say, though, no one could hold a candle to you. You are the picture of loveliness itself."

She flushed at his praise. "Now who is the flatterer?"

He grinned. "It is not flattery if it is true." He leaned down to touch his forehead against hers, his eyes going serious. "I wish you could see yourself through my eyes,

Anne. Never has another man been as fortunate as I am to claim your hand in mine." He lifted their joined hands as proof, then used one hand to twirl a curl that had escaped her braid around his forefinger. "Or to feel the brush of your hair against my skin." He let his gaze linger on her lips. "Or to know the temptation of your kiss."

Those luscious lips parted under his scrutiny, calling him like a siren to a ship full of lonely sailors. He dared to heed that silent appeal, lowering his head to taste of her heady sweetness.

This kiss was different, her promise to be his wife lending their shared embrace an assurance and fervency that had been missing before. Richard slid his hand to cradle the nape of her neck, angling his head to deepen the kiss. His lips sealed his devotion to her. This woman was his. For the rest of their lifetime, her heart would belong only to him and his to her. No other man would have the privilege of claiming her lips with his. That right was his alone.

He let his kiss speak of his pledge to care for her, of all his hope and happiness for their future. Her response echoed his sentiments, chasing away any doubts that might have lingered. Words were superfluous. Their hearts did not need a voice to understand what the other was saying.

They were so involved in their silent communication, they did not realize they had company until Mr. Collins let out a high-pitched squawk and fumbled for purchase on one of the benches near the entrance. "You…you! This is bad. This is very bad!"

Richard raised his mouth from Anne's reluctantly, lifting his head to see what all the fuss was about. He glanced at Mr. Collins, who looked like he was torn between fainting dead away and roaring with outrage. The man's color was high and his hands were shaking. He sputtered, "I cannot believe… Lady Catherine is going to be outraged!"

Richard glanced back at his soon-to-be bride. Her cheeks were becomingly flushed, her lips swollen from his kiss. Her eyes were still slightly dreamy, as if her thoughts still lingered on their kiss, not on Mr. Collins' interruption. He very much wished he could get rid of the obstinate little man so he could go back to kissing her. Instead, he cleared his throat. "Mr. Collins, I do believe you have the wrong impression."

"Do not try to play coy with me! I know what I saw," the scandalized man warned. "You were kissing Miss de Bourgh!" He hiked up his slipping trousers by the belt strap. "I must tell Lady Catherine at once! I know she will not be pleased by such unseemliness going on in her household."

Richard released Anne with a sigh and turned to stalk towards Mr. Collins. Why did such a pleasant interlude have to be so rudely interrupted? It was going to take a monumental effort just to make Mr. Collins see reason, and he would much prefer to be discussing future plans with his wife-to-be, enjoying the tender light in her eyes at the mention of a family of their own.

The parson eyed him warily as he approached, taking a hasty step toward the exit. That small sign of fear made Richard scowl. Did the parson expect him to physically affront him? True, he had been a military man for much of his life, but that did not mean he was violent.

On the contrary, his peaceful disposition had eventually demanded that he resign his position. He sensed Anne taking her place beside him, and reached blindly for her hand, appeased when her slender fingers slipped between his.

He tried to force a smile to his lips and very much feared it came out as a grimace. "Mr. Collins, you are to congratulate us. Miss de Bourgh and I are engaged."

Mr. Collins' gaze flitted between them, as if he was not quite sure he should believe them. "Engaged?"

Anne smiled pleasantly. "Yes, Mr. Collins. Richard has asked for my hand in marriage, and I have agreed."

His eyebrows knit together into a scowl, Mr. Collins asked, "And how does Lady de Bourgh feel about this?"

As if either of them would have come to an agreement without taking Lady Catherine's feelings into consideration. Really. Anne huffed. "My mother has been very eager for me to find a husband and get married, Mr. Collins. I am sure she is overjoyed."

Richard's hand tightened around hers. "Indeed, I have just been to see her myself. She is pleased by the prospect."

Mr. Collins harrumphed, much like Lady Catherine tended to do, and crossed his arms over his chest. "I find that a rather difficult proposition to believe. Lady Catherine would not appreciate losing her only daughter. She would also not be happy to find you taking advantage of her."

Richard fought the urge to roll his eyes. Really. The man was ridiculous. Where was a little of that conciliatory attitude when you needed it? His judgmental tone was taking this conversation a little too far. "I assure you, Mr. Collins, the terms were agreeable to us all." He straightened himself to his full height, snapping his spine into the rigid stance he learned in the military, and looked down his nose at the much smaller man. "And as those terms are between Miss de Bourgh and her family and I, we need not discuss them any further with you."

His irritation must have shown, for Mr. Collins let his hands drop to his sides, shock sliding over his face. He hurried to make amends. "I do apologize, Colonel

Fitzwilliam, er, Mr. Fitzwilliam. And Miss de Bourgh. I never meant to insinuate…That is…"

Anne cut him off with an upraised hand. "That is quite alright, Mr. Collins. There is no harm done. Now, if you will excuse us, Richard and I have much to discuss and a wedding to plan. Unless, of course, there was a reason you were seeking one of us here…" She let her voice trail off pointedly.

"Of course, of course," stammered Mr. Collins. "I was merely checking on you, Miss de Bourgh. I noticed your pony and cart tied up outside and Mr. Fitzwilliam's horse and thought to make sure everything was alright. I take my responsibility toward Lady Catherine very seriously, as you know. I would never want to be accused of shirking my duty."

"Never let it be said so," drawled Richard, tongue smoothly in cheek. "Well, Mr. Collins, your duty has been assuaged. You are free to go about whatever other business keeps you busy this time of day."

Mr. Collins nodded and bowed sharply at the waist, not once, not twice, but three times as he backed toward the door. "As you wish. Miss de Bourgh, Mr. Fitzwilliam. I do hope your marriage is blessed with as much tender affection and bliss as God has seen fit to bestow upon me." With one last ingratiating tilt of his head, he disappeared from view.

Richard gazed at the door that shut behind him thoughtfully. A curl of dread started in his stomach. "You do not suppose he will have to do the wedding, do you?"

Anne burst out laughing. "I suppose he must. Mother will insist upon it, and if we do not want to elope to Gretna Green, I fear it is our only option."

Richard sighed. "I daresay, I do wish I had realized that sooner."

She grinned up at him. "Would it have prevented you from proposing?"

"No," he told her tenderly, reaching up to cup her cheek in the palm of his hand. "However, I might have suggested an immediate trip to Gretna Green."

She giggled, the sound tickling his heart and making his throat tighten with emotion. Her joy was contagious, her ready smile a light to his world. He made it his aim, right then and there, to coax the pleasant sound from her at least once during every day to come.

"It is too late, now. Mother will already be up at the house making plans for the wedding of the century." She leaned her cheek into his palm and smiled up at him, her gaze tender.

He groaned. "I suppose if we are to have any hope of keeping her in check we must go up to the house at once and remind her that this is our wedding, not hers."

"It probably is not a bad idea," Anne agreed, although she was just as reluctant as he was to give up the precious privacy they were currently enjoying.

Richard ran his thumb over her cheekbone, enjoying the way her face flushed at his caress. "I would almost prefer to let her have her way with the wedding if it meant more moments like this."

"I know exactly what you mean," she said softly, reaching up to cradle the hand that still cupped her cheek.

The tender light in her eyes was a blessing he had never expected to see in his lifetime. He had found a part of him he had not known was missing. She was his complement, the piece that completed his puzzle. Without her he would always have been a partial man.

He understood now why Darcy had pushed him to reconcile with Anne. Even if he had not realized it at the time, he would never have lived down that decision. It would have forever haunted him with what-ifs and could-have-beens. Now he did not have to wonder what the future might have held. He would be living his dreams out to the full. Dreams he had not even realized he had before his trip to Rosings without Darcy.

Richard leaned his forehead against hers, letting contentment wash over him. This was exactly where he was supposed to be.

"Richard?" Anne murmured.

"Hmm?" he responded, too blissfully happy to form a coherent sentence.

"My mother will be waiting." Her eyes twinkled up at him.

"Then let her wait." He tugged Anne closer and found her lips with his own. He would not be anywhere else for the world.

CHAPTER TWELVE

They were married three weeks later, in a private ceremony in Rosings' gardens.

Much to Lady Catherine's displeasure, Anne had refused to consider holding the ceremony anywhere else. After much debate, and many reassurances by her daughter and Richard, she had finally relented, telling them with a sniff that is was just as well they had the ceremony here, since Rosings had always been her home.

Her acquiescence on any other number of factors had not been quite so easy to obtain, but still, Richard had to admit, everything had turned out well. He stood beneath an arbor with Mr. Collins and Darcy at his side, awaiting the arrival of his beautiful bride.

He snuck a glance at his cousin, who stood with a ramrod spine and a blank face. He was grateful Darcy had agreed to stand up with him this day. He had not taken that blessing for granted. Lady Catherine and Darcy had reached an uneasy agreement, especially once Lady Catherine had learned of the role Elizabeth had played in convincing her husband to step in for Anne and Richard.

While Lady Catherine had not precisely welcomed the younger woman, she had not been rude either. For the time being, that was enough. Richard was just glad they had managed to put aside their differences long enough to enjoy the day and celebrate their marriage. It would have put a damper on the festivities if the two sides of the family had not been able to be reunited.

Richard let his gaze flit out over the crowd that had gathered to see their nuptials. It was mostly family, really, a much smaller enterprise than Lady Catherine had initially wanted to plan. He knew his bride had had a hand in that. She had no desire to have a big to-do that would tax her energy and patience. She wanted an enjoyable, low key affair that kept the peace and encouraged harmony.

He had come to appreciate that sensible attitude in the last few weeks. He had also come to appreciate and support her forthright opinions. With him to back her up, she was much more comfortable insisting on her own way with her mother, even while she carefully navigated that woman's sensitive feelings.

He was coming to realize there was much to admire about his bride. Oh, he had known there was much to admire already, or he would never have fallen in love with her. But he was realizing it to an even greater extent now. Every day he learned just a little more about her, recognized the hope and promise she brought to his life.

He was one very fortunate man to have her, and he would never, ever forget it.

Elizabeth caught his eye among the seated guests. She gave him an encouraging smile, then her gaze shifted to the man beside him. Darcy raised his chin in response to her raised eyebrow and scowled. She dropped him a saucy wink that teased a reluctant smile to her husband's lips. Seated beside her, his cousin Georgiana watched the interchange with a satisfied smile.

A lot had happened in the past year; a lot of changes had been wrought. Yet, they were all happy ones. The changes were for the better. He prayed that Lady Catherine would realize the truth of that, as everyone else had. And perhaps, when the time came, she would be ready to let go of Anne and let her daughter have her own life and her own family, without feeling the need to control the outcome.

In the meantime, he would be here for Anne, ready to intervene should it be necessary, and always looking out for his wife's best interests.

Mrs. Jenkins, his fiancée's old companion, who had left her a few months earlier to be married herself, preceded her down the aisle, quietly pleased to be able to stand up with her.

A moment later, he caught a glimpse of Anne as she rounded the bend in the garden path. She raised her head and met his gaze, a radiant smile spreading across her features at the sight of him.

She very nearly brought him to his knees. Clad in a simple white gown, her inner beauty shown through. She did not need fancy clothes or complicated hairstyles to make her beautiful, although she had plenty of both. Her lush locks spilled over one shoulder, highlighting her creamy skin and the pink in her cheeks. In her hand she carried a simple bouquet of roses. Her special variety, he knew. She was still deciding on the official name.

Their gazes sought and held over the expanse of people that still separated them.

This was his bride, the woman that would be his wife in only a few more minutes. He itched to go to her, to claim her hand in his, but forced himself to wait patiently as she approached, her arm looped through her mother's as they made their way to him.

He smiled gently at his mother-in-law as she held her head high and sniffed regally. He knew the sheen in her eyes was not from arrogance or pride. It was from the tears she refused to shed. Even Lady Catherine could not remain impassive on a day like today.

He would not want her to be. Anne deserved to know the place she held in her mother's heart, just as she deserved to know the place she held in his. Richard swore to himself never to let her forget it. Day by day, he would be sure that she knew just how special she was to him. No day would pass without a word or gesture on his part reassuring her that she meant the world to him.

Only a few moments more and she was at his side, smiling up at him with a confidence and trust he knew belonged to him. Richard reached out eagerly to take her hand in his, the formality of the wedding ceremony unable to stop him from raising her hand to his lips and pressing a lingering kiss to her smooth skin.

There would be time for the spoken vows later, but right now he wanted her to read his solemn promise in his gaze. No words repeated after Mr. Collins could hold the same veracity as the promise he gave her now. He saw an answering promise in her eyes, a vow that erased any doubts or fears he might still have harbored.

As one, they turned to face the parson, ready to become husband and wife in front of all those who mattered to them the most.

EPILOGUE

Richard glanced up from the ledger in front of him as his wife heaved a frustrated sigh. The ledger open on her desk opposite him was just as thick as his.

"Numbers not adding up?" he asked.

Anne rubbed bleary eyes. She complained, "No, and it is not the first time I have come across a discrepancy. Whoever was caring for these books before us had an appalling head for numbers. Really, it is very simple, basic arithmetic. There is no reason for such blatant mistakes."

Richard chuckled and closed his ledger with a thud. He rose and came around the desks to grasp her hands in his and pull her to her feet. "I think it is time for a break, dearest. I have been staring at those columns of numbers for long enough I am half afraid they are going to leap off the page and start dancing a minuet."

His wife giggled. "Those numbers are not in order enough to follow a simple one-two-three dance pattern."

Richard was inclined to agree. "I did not realize how much work would be involved when my parents offered us the estate. Still, I think it will be well worth the effort in the long run."

Anne nodded. "Undoubtedly. Once we get the property in order, it will be a fine legacy for our family. In the meantime, though, it is quite annoying. Even Rosings was not in such dire straits when I took over the books."

Richard chuckled. "Perhaps, that was because Darcy and I had been handling those matters for you until that point. Whoever was handling these books has obviously not been quite as diligent."

Anne laid her palm against his chest, over the spot where his heart resided, and smiled up at him. His heart picked up pace, thundering away under her hand. Goodness gracious, but that smile got to him every time. Even after a month of marriage, it still turned him to jelly in her hands.

His heart was so loud in his ears he almost did not hear the next words she spoke.

"Nor were they as skilled," she complimented him. "You are a man among men, Richard Fitzwilliam. How in the world did I ever manage to catch your eye?"

Richard smiled. The answer to that question was both simple and complicated. He cupped her face in his hands, letting his gaze settle on her beloved countenance with all the seriousness and adoration he possessed for her. "You did not need to catch my eye," he told her. "You were all I could see from the moment I stepped foot on Rosings."

Her eyes softened and her hand fisted in his shirt, drawing him closer. "You need your eyes checked."

He chuckled, his gaze dropping to her lips. "My eyes are fully functioning, thank you very much, my dear."

His mind, on the other hand, was not. Right now, for instance, it seemed to be fixated on the idea of kissing his wife. And since she was, after all, his wife, he went ahead and gave into the impulse, lowering his head to taste her sweet lips. When he pulled away, Anne's eyes were still closed, her lips parted in a serene smile.

Richard chuckled and ran his thumb over her bottom lip, swollen from his kiss. "Perhaps it is your eyesight I should be questioning. After all, you ended up with a dullard like me."

That brought her eyes open. "Richard!"

She swatted at his chest with faux irritation, but he easily captured her wayward hand in his and brought it back against his chest, cradling her closer.

He leaned his head down to rest his forehead against hers, listening with pleasure to her contented sigh. Life was good. With Anne in his arms, Richard was whole, complete. He could not imagine a moment more perfect than this one, except that they just seemed to keep coming. Over the past month, one perfect moment had led straight into another perfect moment. And that was fine by him. If the rest of his life was filled with moments like this one, he would be a very fortunate man indeed.

He planned to remember every one of them. That way, when the moments came that were not quite so perfect, and Richard was quite sure they would come, he could look back at those memories and be grateful for the gift he had been given.

His dear wife was a gift, a present that no jewels or ornament could adorn any better, and worthy of the utmost adoration. His great respect for her governed the manner in which he tolerated her mother's sometimes high-handed ways and kept him from counting down the days until they might depart Rosings.

At length, Lady Catherine's dearest wish was granted, and they welcomed their firstborn within Rosings walls. This happy event was, of course, accompanied by a more difficult change, as the time had come for their small family to move to a home of their own. Lady Catherine bore this change with begrudging acceptance and a plan to visit often, which, as was her custom, she carried out to the full. Her presence was never entirely unwelcome, for grandchildren softened her in a way motherhood never had, and it was generally accepted that Lady Catherine was a great deal better off for the change than she would have been otherwise.

As for Anne, her health was not always as fair as either she or Richard would have liked, but the fresh country air did her well and in time, her episodes were all but forgotten.

She spent many happy days chasing after her children and tending her roses, filling her life with the kind of light and joy she brought to others.

The story of Pride and Prejudice continues with…
The Children of Pride and Prejudice

Emilia's Folly

PROLOGUE

The flickering firelight in Basil Gilbanks' dimly lit study reflected off the glint of greed in his beady eyes.

"But Pappa, I want the Duke to dance with *me*," Arianna Gilbanks complained, her lower lip extruding in a pout. "I am ten times prettier than that Emilia Wharton. He should be paying his attentions to me, not to a little nobody from the country like her."

Basil Gilbanks regarded his daughter with a calculating gleam in his eye. The dim glow of the fire bathed her features in its warmth, reflecting off her flaxen locks and delicate features, although they were twisted with jealousy at the moment. She was the spitting image of her deceased mother, the very epitome of a diamond of the first waters. His daughter was going to be the means through which he gained a very wealthy and influential son-in-law, preferably someone who would have a little pull with the crown. Maybe even someone who would get a title bestowed on him. Basil Gilbanks had always wanted a title.

His daughter was the envy of every young lady in Town.

Except for one.

Miss Emilia Wharton, lately of Hertfordshire, had come to stay for the Season with the very well-known and respected Bingleys and she was attracting the kind of attention that rightfully belonged to his daughter. Mr. Gilbanks could not stand by idly and allow that to happen. Something had to be done about it.

"I know, my darling girl. You deserve every attention. And we are going to make sure the Duke of Shrewsbury forgets all about Miss Wharton. Just leave it to your Pappa. I will make sure of it."

Basil felt a deep sense of satisfaction at the smile that spread over his daughter's face. She threw her arms around his neck. "I knew I could count on you to get rid of her, Pappa! Tell me, what are you to do?"

Her father shook his head and patted her on the shoulder. "Do not you worry your pretty little head about that, sweetheart. I have it all under control."

She pouted a little that he would withhold the information from her, but she did not truly mind. She was far too pleased to know her rival would be out of the way.

She stood, her problem resolved. "Very well, Pappa, but I want her really and truly taken care of, or I shall be very, very angry."

Basil chuckled at her threats and lifted his cheek for the kiss she bestowed upon it. "Of course, my dear. Now, run along so your dear Pappa may take care of it."

He watched her go fondly, the door clanging shut behind her. He rose and strode to his desk, pulling out his pen and ink and writing a brief note. Upon its completion, he tugged on the bell-pull and waited for the butler to appear in the doorway.

"You rang, sir?"

"Ah, yes, Smoot. Please have this delivered to my stepson at his lodgings. He is to see me at his earliest convenience. I wish for you to make sure the urgency of his response is conveyed to him in the most certain of terms, Smoot, if you take my meaning."

"Of course, Mr. Gilbanks. As you wish." The butler bowed stiffly and left him to see to his wishes.

Basil leaned back in his chair, folding his hands in front of him and resting his chin on his fingers. He smirked, properly pleased with himself.

Emilia Wharton did not stand a chance. He would see her sent back into oblivion if it was the last thing he did.

CHAPTER ONE

Emilia fanned herself with short, irritated flicks of her wrist. The ballroom was crowded with people, the stale stench of unwashed bodies covered by the heady aroma of the latest French perfumes. The smell was nauseating.

The room was warm from the crush of bodies and the heat from the candelabras that were scattered throughout. Another drunken lord bumbled into her, nearly spilling his punch down her gown, and begged her pardon with slurred speech before stumbling off towards the refreshment table.

London was not at all what she had thought it would be.

Aunt Mary's sister, Lydia, had made it sound like such an exciting place, full of glamour and elegance, with sparkling jewels and glittering gowns. To be sure, the first few balls she had attended had been fun, filled with charming conversations and smiling gentlemen plying her for the honor of her hand for a set. But she now realized the Bingleys had been shielding her from the general banality of the Ton, selecting the parties and routs where they could be assured of knowing everyone that was in attendance.

A familiar face appeared before her, bowing over her hand. She smiled up at the Duke of Shrewsbury, relieved it was not another drunken young man come to ask her to take a turn about the terrace.

He greeted her, "Miss Wharton, what a charming surprise to find you here! I did not know the Bingleys were to be in attendance tonight."

"I do not believe it was their intention to do so initially," Emilia said genially. "My dear friend, Olympia Bodham, informed me it was to be the social event of the Season, so I simply insisted that we must be present. The Bingleys were too kind to refuse, I am afraid."

The Duke laughed. "Ah, yes. I believe the Bingleys would never refuse a request if it was within their power to grant it. They are the epitome of kindness itself."

The musicians drew the current song to a close and the dancers clapped before shuffling to new positions- some to new partners, some to the terrace, and some to the refreshment table.

The Duke offered Emilia his hand. "May I have this set?"

Emilia smiled widely at him. "You may." She took his proffered hand and allowed him to lead her on to the dance floor.

A murmur went through the crowd as they took their places amid the other dancers.

"I do believe we have created quite a stir, your Grace," Emilia said with a laugh. "You shall have me in the gossip pages tomorrow morning, I am sure."

"Nonsense," he told her. "I shall be sure to dance with at least two other young ladies after you and the gossip will be diffused."

She giggled. "Be sure that you do, or Uncle Thomas will come to Town in a heartbeat and whisk me back to Hertfordshire."

*****

Arianna Gilbanks snapped her fan closed, a murderous gleam in her eye, and went searching for her Pappa. The man had promised her he was going to take care of this problem, and yet, here Emilia Wharton was, dancing with the Duke for all of London to see!

It was not to be borne! Either she was to dance with the Duke or no one would! Especially not some nobody from Hertfordshire!

Basil Gilbanks saw her coming and steeled himself for his daughter's wrath. His stepson had not responded to his summons as he had expected. He had been forced to seek him out under the guise of attending the ball, but Anthony was nowhere to be seen. It was just like the boy, to show up late just to irk him.

Still, he knew Anthony would show up. As much as he might like to ignore Basil's summons, he never failed to appear when called. He knew what the consequences for his disobedience would be. Basil controlled the purse strings in his family, and there was going to be a nasty surprise for his stepson in the morning if he did not materialize soon.

Arianna stomped to a stop in front of her father. She hissed, "I thought you said you were going to take care of this!"

He hastened to reassure her, "I am, darling. There was a small setback in my plan, but it is nothing to worry about. All will be well soon enough."

She glared at him. "It better be. I should not be made to stand on the outskirts like some wallflower while Miss Wharton dances with *my* Duke!"

Movement at the ballroom's entrance drew Basil's attention from Arianna. He smirked with satisfaction and rubbed his hands together eagerly. He brushed off his daughter. "Now see here, Arianna, I told you I would take care of it, and I will. These things just take a little time. Now, if you want that new dress for the Rycroft's ball next week, you will do well to let me be. Your stepbrother just arrived and I must speak with him."

He left her staring after him, dumbfounded, to approach the main doors. She stomped her foot and whirled away, searching for some hapless debutante to expend her wrath on.

Basil chuckled happily to himself as he neared his stepson, an evil gleam in his eye. This was going to be good, almost too good. He would be rid of both of his problems with one fell swoop.

Sometimes his own brilliance amazed him.

*****

Anthony Fairchild paused on the stairs leading down to the ballroom floor, surveying the room. The couples on the dance floor were a whirl of color and motion, but his gaze sought only one person in particular among the crowd.

He hated his stepfather for demanding his presence, but he hated himself more for capitulating to his demands. He clenched his fists angrily, tension radiating through his neck and shoulders.

He was not sure what Basil Gilbanks wanted with him tonight, but he knew it was not good. It was never good. In the three years since his mother had remarried, Basil had manipulated him into doing many things he was heartily ashamed of. But that was all going to end soon.

His twenty-fifth birthday was nearing, and with it, freedom. The funds his father had put in trust for him would be released to him and he would no longer have to be dependent on that weasel of a man for his every need.

The day could not come soon enough. Unfortunately, it was still about two and a half months off, and so Anthony stood poised on the staircase, searching for the man he detested with the very depths of his being.

He caught movement coming toward him from the corner of his eye and saw his stepfather nearing, grinning from ear to ear.

Basil clapped him on the shoulder, one firm hand turning him toward an alcove. "Ah, Anthony, my good man! I am so glad you could make it." The last of his words came out in an angry hiss. "You certainly kept me waiting long enough."

His stepfather was not happy. Anthony had known he would not be when he had blatantly disregarded his message, but he could not seem to help the small act of defiance, even though he knew he would pay dearly for it on the morrow.

He remained silent, knowing his stepfather would tell him why he had been summoned when he was good and ready. Until then, there was no satisfaction to be gained from interacting with the man. Basil would only toy with him.

Basil pressed him deeper into the alcove, until they could neither be seen nor be heard by those nearby. "I have a job for you."

Anthony fought the urge to roll his eyes. Of course he did. Basil would not have summoned him if he did not have something he wanted him to do.

His stepfather took his silence as acquiescence. Which, to be honest, was a fairly accurate assessment. Anthony did not have the means to deny him anything.

"I mean for the Duke of Shrewsbury to marry your sister, Arianna." The smile he bestowed on Anthony was oily and sly. "She shall make a most becoming Duchess, will she not?"

His stepfather might try to appeal to Anthony's sense of familial obligation, but he would never claim that shrew as his sister. Nonetheless, he grunted his begrudging agreement.

"And you shall help me accomplish my task."

Ah, finally, they had reached the crux of the matter. He managed to grind out between his teeth, "And how am I to do that?"

Basil chuckled hollowly. "His Grace has been distracted lately from his pursuit of your sister by a cunning little minx from the country, a Miss Emilia Wharton. I want her out of the way."

Anthony nearly choked. "Surely, you do not mean for me to kill her!"

"Of course not! I am not that heartless!" Basil grumbled irritably beneath his breath, something about his imbecile of a stepson. "I mean for you to compromise her! Send her back into the countryside in shame!"

Anthony was stunned speechless. His stepfather continued rambling on, but Anthony heard nothing that followed. He could not be serious! To jeopardize his own happiness and future so Arianna could secure herself a husband? It was preposterous! No self-respecting woman, much less one Anthony would be interested in pursuing, would consider him as a match with such a past hanging over his head.

"You must be joking," he bit out frostily, interrupting Basil's gleeful monologue. "I will do no such thing."

Basil's eyes hardened. "You will, or your funds will dry up by tomorrow and you will spend the rest of your life in the duns."

Anthony stiffened at the threat, but refused to bow to his wishes. Basil had gone too far this time. This was a woman's reputation they were talking about, something to be guarded and protected, not thrown away.

Basil's gaze sharpened. "Think you are so high and mighty now, do you? Too good for me, are you? Fine, I will sweeten the pot. I know your weakness, Anthony Fairchild."

Alarm coursed through Anthony's veins. Basil could not possibly know…

"Briarwick Manor."

Anthony's heart stuttered to a stop. He bit out angrily, "You would not!"

But he would. Basil's eyes gleamed with satisfaction. "See to it, and it is yours once the deed is done. Refuse me, and I will sell it to the highest bidder."

Anthony clenched his jaw. Briarwick Manor had been home to the Fairchilds for generations. His father had meant for the property to continue on as a home for his beloved wife after his passing and then for it to pass to Anthony, but upon her remarriage it had fallen into Basil's greedy fingers. Unfortunately, he knew how much the property meant to Anthony.

It was his home; the place of so many of his happy childhood memories, and the place he had one day dreamed of returning to in order to start his own family.

There was no choice. As much as he might hate himself for it, he would never forgive himself if he lost his family's birthright. If he was to redeem Briarwick Manor, he had to do Basil's bidding.

He forced himself to speak. "I do not know this Emilia Wharton of whom you speak. How can I possibly do as you ask?"

Basil cackled and pulled him forward. "And you thought you could deny Basil Gilbanks!" He pointed out over the crowd on the dance floor. "See there, the Duke of Shrewsbury? Dancing with him is your quarry, Emilia Wharton."

Anthony followed the line of Basil's finger, his gaze skipping over the well-known Duke of Shrewsbury to land on his partner.

Anthony caught a glimpse of her face and forgot to breathe. *Surely not.* But it was. He would have recognized her anywhere.

Other books by Lelia M. Silver

The story of Pride and Prejudice continues with…
The Children of Pride and Prejudice series

Emilia's Folly

John's Downfall

Sophia's Champion

Thea's Legacy

Helene's Honor

Hannah's Viscount

Theo's Choice

Eliza's Journey

Pride and Prejudice goes for a spin in the Old West with…
Pemberley Creek series

Pride and Presumption

Pride and Perfection

A modern twist to Pride and Prejudice

Pride and Precipice

9 781965 406038